Weekend in VEGAS

Four friends, four dream weddings!

On a girly weekend in Las Vegas, best friends Alex, Molly, Serena and Jayne are just supposed to let their hair down and forget men—but they end up meeting their perfect matches! Will the love they find in Vegas stay in Vegas?

Find out in this sassy, fun and wildly romantic miniseries all about love and friendship!

Dear Reader,

Las Vegas is a city that practically explodes with sights, sounds and sensation. Everything happens fast. It's exciting…and in most cases, very temporary.

That was what Alexandra Lowell, was expecting. She was going to Las Vegas for a short, no-regrets weekend with her friends.

But then trouble came calling. Wyatt McKendrick, a rich, gorgeous loner, stepped in and made her an offer she couldn't refuse. One that would keep her in the city temporarily. Fighting her attraction to him all the way.

So I had to wonder… What would happen when the hourglass emptied and these two allergic-to-love people finally said goodbye? Maybe…nothing? No love, no harm done?

Hmm, that *could* happen—but this is *Las Vegas,* where the impossible becomes possible, and things a girl never imagined happening…happen. Even love.

Myrna Mackenzie

MYRNA MACKENZIE

Saving Cinderella!

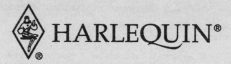

TORONTO • NEW YORK • LONDON
AMSTERDAM • PARIS • SYDNEY • HAMBURG
STOCKHOLM • ATHENS • TOKYO • MILAN • MADRID
PRAGUE • WARSAW • BUDAPEST • AUCKLAND

Recycling programs
for this product may
not exist in your area.

ISBN-13: 978-0-373-17665-6

SAVING CINDERELLA!

First North American Publication 2010.

Copyright © 2010 by Myrna Topol.

Myrna Mackenzie grew up not having a clue what she wanted to be (she hadn't been born a princess, the one job she thought she might like, because of the steady flow of pretty dresses and crowns), but she knew that she loved stories and happy endings, so falling into life as a romance writer was pretty much inevitable. Now an award-winning author, Myrna was born in a small town in Dunklin County, Missouri, grew up just outside Chicago and now divides her time between two lakes in Chicago and Wisconsin, both very different and both very beautiful. She adores the Internet (which still seems magical after all these years), loves coffee, hiking, "attempting" gardening (without much success), cooking and knitting. Readers (and other potential gardeners, cooks, knitters, writers, etc.) can visit Myrna online at www.myrnamackenzie.com or write to her at P.O. Box 225, La Grange, IL 60525.

PROLOGUE

ALEXANDRA LOWELL stared up at the shining façade of McKendrick's of Las Vegas, the most exclusive hotel she would probably ever enter in her life, and hoped that this weekend wasn't a mistake. Her bank account was practically sobbing at the expense, but her friend Jayne was in desperate straits and in need of some serious escapism, so Alex was going to forget about that poor bank account. For now.

She smiled at her three friends. "I'm setting my mental countdown clock. We're going to have one awesome weekend in an alternative universe," she told them cheerfully.

Serena chuckled. "Alternative universe, Alex? It's Las Vegas, not another planet."

Alex gave her friend a patient smile. "Serena, come on. You've been in my apartment. I love it to pieces, I love finally having my own home, but it's a little box. This is…it's…"

"An alternative universe," Molly agreed with a laugh.

"Okay, you're right," Serena said. "This place *is* breathtaking, isn't it? Look at all these people, the bustle, the sounds, the over-the-top opulence of it all."

"And we've got a whole weekend," Jayne said. "Darn it, we're going to have fun, aren't we?"

Her smile was bright, but Alex knew she was only wearing

it for their benefit. Jayne was supposed to have been getting married this weekend, but that wasn't happening. Alex's heart hurt for her. Friends just didn't let friends go through heartbreak alone. Friends did everything possible to cheer each other up.

"Absolutely," Alex agreed. "This was a great idea, Serena." Serena had been the one to suggest a Las Vegas escape, and already the excitement of an adventure was starting to build until Alex could barely contain herself.

"So…do you think it's true that lots of unmentionably wild things happen here?" Molly asked.

"I certainly hope so," Jayne said with dogged determination. "We deserve a little wildness. For this weekend, San Diego and everyone in it ceases to exist."

Which was fantastic advice, Alex couldn't help thinking. Jayne wasn't the only one at a turning point in her life. Alex had her own issues she wanted left at home.

"Absolutely," Molly said. "The only people who matter this weekend are you, my very best friends. We're out to set the world on fire."

"And no regrets," Serena said. "When we remember this time, I want us to have major grins on our faces."

"When we leave here," Alex declared, "we're only taking one thing with us—a happy glow. We're never going to look back and question the choices we made this weekend."

With those words, they all smiled at each other and marched toward their destinies.

CHAPTER ONE

SATURDAY afternoon, Alex, tired but glowing from the spa, shopping, dining and partying they'd crammed in to their weekend, dashed downstairs for a souvenir menu from Sparkle, the rooftop restaurant. Tomorrow she and her friends would leave Las Vegas, and who knew if she'd ever return? But one look at the heavily pregnant concierge's face and she knew something was wrong.

Still, the woman pasted on a weak smile. "May I help you?" she asked, her voice a thin thread.

Alex hesitated. The woman's smile was fake, but it would be intrusive to ask questions, wouldn't it? Alex reminded herself that in the past her habit of rushing in to help without being asked had resulted in her being told to mind her own business. Or worse. She tried to bar the painful memory of what had happened some of the other times she'd overstepped the boundaries. But dwelling on her past mistakes wasn't helping this situation. The woman still looked distressed, and…

"I'm sorry," Alex said. "I don't mean to be nosy, but I can tell something's wrong. Is there anything I can do to help? Someone I can call?"

The woman's eyes widened. "No! You're a guest! I mean…I'm fine. Just a little tired."

Instantly Alex felt both guilty that she'd made the woman uncomfortable, and chagrined that she'd once again made the mistake of pushing too hard. So many of the painful moments in her life had begun with her trying to help too much. The memory of her latest doomed relationship nagged at her.

Stop it, she ordered herself. *Apologize for making this woman uncomfortable and go. Don't think about the mistakes you've made.*

The concierge suddenly let out a gasp, pulling Alex back to the present. She glanced down and realized that with her attention elsewhere, she'd missed something major. Pressed close against the desk with her arms folded in front of her, the woman had managed to—mostly—disguise the fact that she was pregnant. Immediately every other thought Alex had vanished. This woman was in real distress. That was a total game changer. No hesitating allowed.

"Forget that I'm a guest," Alex said. "Who would you like me to call?"

The woman looked like a *Vogue* cover model, her hair and make-up perfect, but her eyes were incredibly round and scared. "I—I don't know. I—" She had risen and was looking at her belly. "It's not supposed to be happening. I have four more weeks, and—I'm not ready. *We're* not ready. I need someone to watch my son, and I promised my boss, Wyatt, that I had weeks before he'd need a replacement. It can't be time yet."

But it was, and clearly something needed to be done.

"I'm sure Wyatt will understand," Alex said.

The woman looked at her as if she were insane. "Wyatt likes things orderly. No messes or craziness."

Well, then, Wyatt certainly wouldn't like *her,* Alex couldn't help thinking. She ignored that thought. Wyatt, whoever he was, wasn't her concern. "Are you in pain?"

"No. Yes. I feel strange. Different than last time. Things feel…faster. But I have another hour to work. Lois, the night concierge, isn't due back from her vacation until tomorrow, so Wyatt can't even find a sub for me today. I really need to stay." She gasped and put a hand on her back.

Somehow Alex hid her own distress. "Don't worry— Belinda," she said, reading the nameplate on the woman's desk. "I'm trained in basic emergency procedures and I'll help you. Would you feel more comfortable sitting? You don't have to stand for my sake."

The woman's eyes grew wider. "I…can't sit. I'll get the chair wet. My water…"

"Don't worry about the chair," Alex said, circling the desk. "You need to get off your feet."

The woman sat. Her perfect skin turned pale.

"Do you have your doctor's number?"

"In my wallet. In my purse. In the drawer."

In mere seconds Alex had the information and placed the call. She spoke to the receptionist, gave her Belinda's name, and received instructions. She called over a young man from the registration desk and asked him to locate his boss.

"Your boss will need to find someone to take Belinda's place. She's going to the hospital."

The young man looked at Belinda's stricken face.

"Randy, I know how important these next few weeks are to Wyatt," the woman said, her voice breathless and strained. "It's awards season. Reviewers will be visiting. A whole series of them. And they'll be anonymous. We can't let down our guard."

"I'm sure Wyatt will understand," Alex said, even though she didn't know any such thing. She sent the young man scurrying to call his boss.

The woman let out a cry. "Breathe," Alex instructed, her voice gentle but firm. "Forget the hotel. Breathe out."

Belinda obeyed. Alex knelt at her side, held her hand, and began to coach her through the pain.

An expensively dressed woman appeared at the desk, her expression uncertain. "The Bistro Lizette?"

Belinda was bent over. Alex reached out and grabbed a map off the desk, glancing at it. "Second floor, west wing. I've been there. You'll love it." She smiled, sending the woman away.

In the distance an ambulance could be heard. Alex wondered what her friends would think of this.

As another person appeared, she gave him instructions and sent him on his way, but she couldn't help noting that the man at the front desk looked concerned.

"Wyatt's on the way," he said, appearing at Alex's side as she began to coach Belinda through another contraction. "Maybe you should move out of the public eye. This hotel is Wyatt's baby. No pun intended."

"Leave Wyatt to me," Alex said. "She's in pain. I'm not moving her until the ambulance arrives."

She certainly hoped this Wyatt person didn't give Belinda grief for not timing her baby's arrival better. She also hoped he wasn't that tall, gorgeous, intimidating man in the suit who had just entered the lobby and turned in her direction.

Wyatt headed across the lobby toward the concierge's desk. There, two EMTs were placing his very pregnant concierge on a stretcher. A slender woman with long dark hair smiled at her, took her hand, and turned to a man who had neared the desk. The man nodded, took the map the woman had obviously given him, and backed away from the area.

"I've called your husband and directed him to meet you at

the hospital. Your neighbor will watch your son. I'll handle things until someone comes," the woman told Belinda, her calm, clear voice softened by distance. "Don't worry. Everything's under control."

At that moment Randy at the front desk saw Wyatt and headed him off. "Wyatt, I tried to get the woman to move Belinda to somewhere less public. People are staring. But she told me that if you were upset she would handle you—just as cool as you please."

Wyatt raised an eyebrow. Because of his height and his high expectations of himself and others he had a tendency to intimidate. Women—people—didn't offer to *handle* him, as a rule. The fact that this one had made her…interesting.

As he watched, a woman in a flowered blouse started toward the empty registration desk, frowned, and turned in his direction. But after one look at Wyatt, and at Randy's scowl, she headed toward the woman with Belinda. The still smiling, calm woman, Wyatt couldn't help noting.

He should step in. Help. It was what he would have normally done, but…not yet. The EMTs were questioning Belinda, and the woman taking her place… He had to see what happened. If necessary, he would do damage control.

As he watched, the guest in the flowered blouse began to apologize profusely, explaining how she had overflowed the bathtub, but the dark-haired woman smiled sweetly, took one fleeting look at Belinda and picked up the phone.

"Please don't worry," she told the woman, writing down her room number. "It's being taken care of. Please let us know if you have any other problems."

The woman with the plumbing problem clutched her savior's hand, thanking the dark-haired beauty.

Correction, he thought. *Beauty* wasn't the right word,

exactly. The woman wasn't classically pretty, but there was something in her manner that gave the illusion of beauty. Despite this odd situation, she acted as if she did this kind of thing every day. And when Belinda moaned, she offered soothing words with what seemed like genuine concern.

Belinda's moan had an effect on him, too. She was too pale, suffering. He had to help. "Call the main office and have them send anyone who can spare a few minutes to help during their breaks," he told Randy. "I will, of course, pay them double time for the minutes they give up. We'll manage to cover. For today, anyway," he said, striding toward Belinda.

"Wyatt, I'm sorry," Belinda said as he reached her, and took her hand.

"For creating a life? Nothing to be sorry for."

"But my replace—" A long, anguished moan escaped her.

Wyatt's whole body reacted to her pain. "She's all right?" he asked one of the EMTs.

"She's having a baby, man, but everything looks good," the man said. "Pain's part of the process."

"Do *not* think about McKendrick's," he told Belinda. "That's an order. I found a replacement this morning."

At his words Belinda smiled weakly. "You found someone? Good. I can go now," she told the EMT. Then she turned to the dark-haired woman. "Thank you for keeping me sane."

"Thank *you*," the woman said. "It's not every day I get to do something so satisfying."

As the EMTs pushed Belinda away, the woman started toward the elevators.

Wyatt reached her in three long strides. "Excuse me, but who in blazes *are* you?"

She stopped, staring up at him with eyes the color of sky. With her full attention concentrated on him, he felt as if a great big fist of awareness had hit him square in the chest. Who on earth had eyes that blue?

"No one," she said.

For a moment Wyatt thought she was answering his question about her eyes…until he realized that she was telling him who she was. "I'm just a guest who was in the lobby when Belinda's labor pains started. No big deal." She started to leave.

"No big deal? Sorry, but…no. I own this place, and it was a very big deal to me. Whoever you are, you're not 'no one'. You handled a woman in labor, a very flustered Randy, the concierge desk of an unfamiliar hotel, and you managed to soothe a nervous guest all at the same time. No guests were harmed or inconvenienced, and the flow of the hotel was largely uninterrupted. Tell me, Miss…*no one*, do you do this kind of thing often?"

For some reason that finally seemed to fluster her. "Not exactly *this* kind of thing, this baby thing, but unfortunately, yes, I have a tendency to jump into these kinds of situations. I once tried to give someone CPR, only to discover that the victim was part of a group of amateur filmmakers making a movie. It was embarrassing for me and frustrating for them."

Her voice was low. She frowned. "I don't regret helping Belinda. The worst kind of ogre would have stepped in. But that other stuff…interfering with your customers…I really didn't even stop to think. I may have given out some incorrect information, and you probably already have some emergency system set up. Some protocol that should have been followed. No wonder that guy at the desk was so irritable."

She looked up at him, those sky eyes looking slightly vulnerable. An intense awareness of her as an attractive woman, not just as a woman who had helped his employee and his hotel, swept through Wyatt. He frowned. Guests were off-limits.

He shook his head. "I'm glad you didn't hesitate. You kept things running and helped Belinda cope. From what I could see, and what Randy said, you took charge of a difficult situation with calm efficiency." His tone brooked no argument.

She gave a low, delicious laugh. "Do you think I could get that in writing? I know I got rather bossy with Randy, and other than getting medical help for Belinda, some people would call what I did sticking my nose in where it didn't belong. Did I really act as if it was perfectly normal for me to field a question about plumbing? I hope that problem got taken care of by the right people. If it did, then I'm just glad that things worked out and nothing too terrible happened. Anyway, now you can get back to making your guests happy," she said with a smile. "It really *is* a beautiful hotel."

She patted his arm, as if he was another guest who needed soothing. For some reason that bothered him. Which was ridiculous. What this woman thought of him was immaterial. He never let others' opinions of him matter. Except where McKendrick's reputation was concerned.

Which brought him full circle to what was really important. This woman had kept things from getting out of control. She'd impressed him in a way none of the temps he'd interviewed had been able to. How had she managed it so effortlessly?

Wyatt didn't know, but he intended to find out. With Belinda's departure, the time for contemplation had passed. In his line of work, the difference between a good businessman and a mediocre one was knowing when to be bold. The door opportunity had opened could suddenly slam shut.

"Excuse me, Miss…?"

"Lowell. Alexandra Lowell. But almost everyone calls me Alex."

Almost everyone. For half a second he wondered if those who didn't fall into that category were men. No matter. He cleared his throat. "Alex. All right. If you don't mind my asking, what do you do for a living?"

Those big blue eyes blinked. "I work the front desk of a chain hotel and run a Web site promoting the sights and sounds of San Diego."

"Ah." That explained things a little. She already had some of the skills a good concierge possessed. While he, he reminded himself, had an empty concierge desk and no prospects in sight.

That was a problem. McKendrick's was known for its opulence, its attention to detail and, above all, its service. This hotel was the project that had saved Wyatt's life. He'd built it from the ground up and poured his soul into it during the dark days, when he'd come to a fork in the road and realized that if he didn't channel his anger into a meaningful goal, he would destroy himself.

These days the resort was a well-oiled machine, but even well-oiled machines could break down without care. A few customers without access to a competent concierge to pamper them could flood the review Web sites and do a lot of damage. Losing Belinda left a hole in customer service that needed to be filled immediately. He could run interference and handle some of her duties, but not all the time. Besides, some guests found him intimidating. He needed to take action. Now.

Wyatt glanced at Alex, a woman guests apparently warmed to, one used to directing people to the local sights and sounds, albeit those of a different city. None of the candidates he'd interviewed thus far could have done what Alex had done. His instincts were urging him to make a move.

Still he resisted. She was a total unknown, who claimed she had a tendency to rush in to help people. That meant she could be emotional, which could mean trouble. And she had those incredible vulnerable eyes that he found far too attractive.

"If you run a Web site, I assume you're comfortable with Internet research?" he said, probing.

"The web is my weakness," she confessed. "McKendrick's site, by the way, has some great features. The virtual tour of the restaurants and clubs is amazing…although a menu for the ice cream bar at the Slide Pool would be helpful. That is, if you're looking for suggestions." She looked suddenly uncomfortable. "I— Please forget I said that. I apologize if I was rude."

The woman just offered you a suggestion on how to improve the hotel Web site, McKendrick. At least interview her, his instincts screamed.

Okay, no avoiding the obvious. Despite his flaws and the mistakes he'd made in his life, he had an unerring instinct about what worked for McKendrick's. He'd made a fortune following his gut feelings. Randy had been a spontaneous hire, driven purely by instinct, but Wyatt had never regretted the decision. Besides, with Belinda gone he couldn't afford more time interviewing people who couldn't handle the job. And this *was* Las Vegas. Fast. Temporary. A person you met today might be gone two hours from now. And Alex was a guest. Just passing through.

"I wonder—do you have a minute to step into my office?" he asked suddenly. "I have some questions."

Now she looked wary. "I have friends waiting."

He nodded. "Five minutes? It's important."

Still she hesitated.

For a second he thought he heard her mutter something under her breath about the wisdom of counting to ten. But then she nodded. "All right. After all, what difference can five minutes make?"

A lot, Wyatt thought. A lot could happen, and he had plenty of experience about all the bad things. This time, however, he was hoping for something more positive.

CHAPTER TWO

WYATT glanced at Alex as they moved down the hallway toward his office. She was tall and willowy and…restless. Moments earlier she had excused herself to make a call.

"My apologies for stealing you away from your friends," he said.

"I just had to let them know where I am. They were expecting me several minutes ago. But since I'm here…could you help me forward a card to Belinda? Babies are important."

"Do you have children of your own?" he asked.

"No. I'm not married."

Wyatt felt his senses go on full alert, coupled with a slight sense of relief—no doubt a knee-jerk reaction to the fact that this beauty hadn't been claimed. But there was also wariness *because* she hadn't been claimed. He'd never allow himself to pursue a woman who wanted children. His kind didn't promise forever, so they didn't produce babies.

No matter. She would either say yes to what he was about to propose, and their new relationship would create distance between them, or she would say no and he'd never see her again.

Five minutes, he reminded himself, opening the door of his office. "Have a seat."

She looked at the leather chair as if it might have sharp teeth hiding beneath the upholstery.

"Problem?"

"No. I was just thinking that I feel a bit like a kid who's unexpectedly been sent to the principal's office. Mr.— Mr....?"

"McKendrick. Wyatt McKendrick."

"Of course. Mr. McKendrick. I'm not sure what this is about, but I have to tell you that I'm pretty uncomfortable."

"And frank."

She shrugged. "That's me." But, despite her discomfort, she sat. She was wearing a white dress, and he couldn't help noticing that she had amazing legs. He frowned at his reaction.

"Total honesty *does* bother some people," she conceded, and he realized that she had noticed his frown.

Wyatt shook his head. "Honesty is..." *What I demand of my employees*, he'd meant to say. But he didn't want to come on too strong. Starting with employee rules would be the wrong approach. "I'll make this brief, Alex. I'm sure you could see how concerned Belinda was about her replacement."

Alex looked wary. "Ye-es."

"She takes her work very seriously, and she excels at it."

"A good concierge must be hard to find."

"Yes. The job requires someone who can think on her feet."

"Of course."

"Someone who knows how to make customers feel at ease, who makes them feel that their concerns matter, whether they need tickets to a show or have a plumbing problem."

She blinked. Wyatt supposed the plumbing comment had been too much, since she'd handled such a problem only minutes earlier. But he didn't have any time to waste. She was a guest here. Temporary.

"Of course a good concierge also knows every detail of the city, but that can be learned," he said.

Alex frowned. "I don't understand. Why are you telling me this?"

"I find myself temporarily short a concierge."

"You told Belinda you'd hired someone."

"I lied. She would have worried, and right now she needs to concentrate on herself and her family."

A small, pretty smile turned Alex's extraordinary face even more intriguing. "You don't sound like the ogre Randy made you out to be."

He raised one eyebrow.

A guilty flush coloured her cheeks. "Forget I said that."

"Already forgotten. Randy, for all his fussing, is good at what he does."

"And as the owner of this…palace of a hotel," she said, "that's very important to you?"

"Absolutely. I only want the best people."

Suddenly she looked more relaxed. "Good. For a minute I was worried. It almost sounded as if you were going to offer me a job."

"I am. I need a sub for Belinda." He surprised himself by blurting it out. Even though he was in a bit of a bind, he'd still intended to give the issue a little more thought. Do a quick background check. No matter. All that could be done after the fact.

"You can't be serious. I've never been a concierge."

"And I'd never owned a hotel until this one. Some people are naturals."

"You know nothing about me."

"I know enough. And I'll find out the rest."

"I could be a total idiot."

"No. You couldn't."

"I could be a thief."

He shook his head. "I don't think so."

She gave him the kind of look people reserved for small boys who were trying to snow them. "I *could* live in San Diego." She glanced at him from beneath very long lashes. Her expression clearly said, *Give me an answer for that.*

Wyatt allowed himself the smallest of smiles. "You mentioned that. San Diego's a beautiful city."

"I know. I love it."

"And…you're not interested in relocating."

"I'm sorry. No. I'm invested in the city. In addition to my Web site, *San Diego Your Way*, I'm hoping to open a shop of the same name soon. So, while I'm flattered that you would offer to hire me, references unseen, I can't move."

Okay, this was going to be difficult. But then he'd been raised in difficult circumstances. Horrible circumstances involving beating and ego-killing insults. Situations that were merely difficult didn't faze him at all.

"You couldn't be persuaded to relocate even for a few months?"

Alex shook her head, her sable hair brushing her cheeks. "I'm sorry. It wouldn't be practical. I have a job."

"At the front desk of a hotel chain. I take it that you already have the capital to open your shop? I see." What he didn't see was why the thought of letting Alex slip away bothered him. He hadn't laid eyes on her fifteen minutes ago.

The best reason he could give for this odd crestfallen sensation was that McKendrick's was his life. Making it the best it could be, aiming to get it on every five-star list, was what drove him. Anything that negatively affected McKendrick's messed with his life and his plans for the future. Given that, Alex had seemed like a gift. That must be why he felt let down.

She had ducked her head, refusing to look directly at him for the first time since they'd begun their conversation. "Well, I'm not actually close to having the capital. It's expensive living in California. But I'm working on it and getting closer."

Alex sounded so apologetic that Wyatt wanted to smile. As if the state of the economy was her fault. Still, he saw one last opportunity—one he would grasp. He'd been called a lone wolf before, a man with no ties, one who followed the scent of whatever he wanted, relentlessly. It was an apt description. He needed to succeed, and right now he felt the thrill of having discovered Alexandra's weak spot.

"So if I offered you a better salary—" he named an amount large enough that Alex jerked her head up "—and promised to find you work equivalent to what you've been doing if this doesn't work out, or when you return to San Diego in two months, even that wouldn't convince you to become my concierge?"

Somehow that last phrase had come out a bit wrong: too sensual, too possessive. Dammit, it had sounded as if he was offering to put her up as his mistress.

And she was looking like a pretty sable rabbit that wanted to take the bait but was wary of anything offered by a wolf.

Suddenly she looked him square in the eyes, rose to her feet and smiled. The pretty rabbit disappeared, replaced by a very human, very lovely woman. "This is very tempting and totally unexpected. When I came downstairs today I was looking for a menu, not a job. I love my home. I have friends there that I don't want to give up. I have hopes and dreams, and all of them are based in San Diego."

That statement alone should have sent chills down his spine. People who used the term *hopes and dreams* tended to be breakable people. He steered clear of them.

"Your…dreams," he said, "may be centered in San Diego but taking this job would help you reach your goals much more quickly. You could raise the capital you need."

She closed her eyes.

"What are you doing?" he asked.

She didn't answer at first. For a second he thought he heard her counting beneath her breath. He *did* hear her counting. But when she got to six, she opened her eyes.

"What am I doing? I'm trying not to say yes," she said with a groan. "I need time. Because if I make the wrong decision we might both regret it. This whole situation…it's completely crazy. I just came here for the weekend. I have friends I'm flying back with."

"I'll refund the price of your airline ticket."

She raised her brows. "Somehow that won't solve the problem."

"Problem?"

"I have a reputation for jumping into fires that burn me. I promised myself I'd stop that. Agreeing to do this… I mean, just look at you."

Wyatt waited. She clearly had more to say.

"I can hear their thoughts already. Some good-looking resort owner asks Alex to please help him and what does she do? She leaps right in. They'll think I've lost my mind. I— no. I need to be smart."

Don't push her, Wyatt told himself. Hadn't everything she'd told him indicated that she had a tendency to let her emotions guide her? No matter what his gut instincts were saying, that wasn't what he was looking for. He'd had a lifetime of bad experiences with people whose emotions dictated their actions, and up until he was old enough to be on his own he'd been forced to suffer the bitter consequences.

Still, this was short-term work they were discussing.

"A sensible person trying to save money would go for the gold, wouldn't she?" Wyatt asked.

Alex frowned. "Maybe she would. But I... This is a big step. I really should go. I'll need to think this through."

Before he could say one word, she had moved to the door.

"Alex?" he said, before the door had opened an inch.

She turned to look at him.

"Don't think it through too much," he said. "Stay here. I'll make it worth your while."

A woman—someone other than Alex—gasped. Alex swung the door wide to reveal three women. Wyatt wanted to groan. He was very careful to keep his personal and business life separate. In fact, he'd opted not to *have* much of a personal life.

Alex was blushing prettily, but she held her chin high. "Jayne, Serena, Molly—meet Wyatt McKendrick, my potential new boss. Wyatt, these are my best friends."

And obviously very protective of Alex, from the looks of them. He nodded to the three openly curious women. "It's very nice to meet you. I'm hoping that Alex will make me a very happy innkeeper. I need her."

Wrong thing to say. Her friends' expressions said that he was a wolf and Alex was a tasty lamb. They would try to convince her not to take the position.

But he was determined to have her. It wasn't just the way she'd handled Belinda's situation and the customers. It was how she'd stood up to *him*. Not many people dared to question him. She was brave without being overbearing. It was a good quality for a concierge.

Or a woman. He frowned at that out-of-place thought and, leaning down, whispered in Alex's ear, upping the salary he had proposed earlier. "I really do need help," he said.

"What did he whisper to you?" one of her friends asked. Good. They were looking out for her. He liked his employees to have strong support systems. He'd grown up without one, so he didn't require one, but most people did. It made for a happy, productive employee.

Still, he was on a mission. "How much time do you need?"

"I leave tomorrow afternoon."

"Then think it over tonight. I'll meet you here tomorrow morning at eight. And...Alexandra?"

The startled look in her eyes told him that *very* few people called her by her full name. Good.

She waited.

"Say yes," he told her.

"You might regret it," she said, "but I'll consider it."

Was she right? Would he regret being hasty? Most likely. Alex Lowell was very appealing. That could be a problem. He didn't make personal connections, and that was an unbreakable rule. Yes, he would regret pursuing Alex.

But he would also regret *not* pursuing her. He only hired the best, and his infallible instinct, which had enabled a rebellious, angry young man to build an empire out of nothing, told him that she *was* the best.

And he wanted her.

CHAPTER THREE

ALEX felt as if she'd just jumped out of an airplane and realized she didn't know how to pull the cord on her chute.
A thousand questions were firing in her brain as she and her
friends headed to her room. What had just happened? She
had expected Wyatt to ask her to give him a play-by-play
of her experience with Belinda. Instead he'd offered her a
job and an obscene amount of money. She remembered that
much. But mostly she remembered how every time Wyatt
had looked at her, her entire body had reacted as if she'd
just discovered, at age twenty-eight, the difference between
men and women. And why some women got into hair-
pulling contests over a virile man or tattooed men's names
on their bodies.

Wyatt was going to be a problem. And not because of anything *he* would say or do. Oh, no.

It was all her. *She* was the problem. The man made her
hands shake with awareness of her body. She'd practically had
to sit on them to keep them still, and she couldn't have that.
Her relationships with men had always been awful, starting
with her father's and stepfather's abandonment of her. She still
remembered running after her stepfather's car, begging him
to stop. It had been the beginning of a life of over-achievement,

of volunteering to help men with their problems, only to get her heart broken. But her last awful experience with Michael had been the worst. A child had been harmed by that relationship, so she was through. And since she loved being independent with no need of a man, her instant reaction to Wyatt should have been a blaring warning that she was in danger of making a major mistake. The only sensible thing to do in such a situation was—

"Run back to San Diego." She muttered the words beneath her breath.

"What did you say?" Molly asked.

"I said that you don't have to worry about me," she told her friends as they entered the hotel room she was sharing with Jayne. The truth was that she could handle the worrying about herself part of things just fine.

"You can't come to Las Vegas for a weekend and end up staying," Jayne said. "Alex, that's insane. You could get hurt."

Alex shook her head. "No, I can't. I have new rules for myself. Parameters. If I took this, it would be just a job." *One she'd have turned down instantly if Wyatt hadn't made it difficult to say no.* "I love your hair, by the way."

Alex, Molly and Serena had pitched in to give Jayne a salon treatment, and she'd had her waist-length hair cut short. Alex knew it was because Jayne's fickle fiancé had loved her long hair.

"Thank you, but that won't work," Jayne said.

"What won't?" As if Alex didn't understand.

"She means that you can't distract us," Molly said, frowning. "Alex, we're worried about you. We know running into Michael and his daughter hurt you last week. If you stay here alone…well, we don't want you to stay here alone."

Alex's throat began to close up. Molly, Serena and Jayne had been there for her when Michael had broken her heart and her spirit. They'd had her back...always.

"Thank you, but don't worry. I haven't decided yet what I'm doing."

"Decide no," Serena said. "This is too big a change to make so quickly."

"Yes, it is," Alex agreed. "I totally agree."

Jayne and Molly and Serena looked at each other.

"You're going to do it, aren't you?" Serena asked.

"I probably shouldn't, but when he was whispering to me..."

Alex's breath caught at the memory of Wyatt's breath lifting her hair, tickling her ear.

Molly snapped her fingers in front of Alex's face. "Come back, Alex."

Alex blinked. "I wasn't daydreaming. I was thinking."

"About...?" Jayne prompted.

"She was thinking about Mr. McKendrick whispering in her ear. In that very sexy way," Serena said.

Serena didn't miss a trick. It was best not to let anyone focus too much on how irresistibly sexy Wyatt was.

"This has nothing to do with Mr. McKendrick's hotness factor. The thing is...he offered me three times my current salary," Alex said. "Then he upped it again."

Jayne's eyebrows rose. "I think we better sit down while you tell us what happened. You only stepped out to get a menu."

"Talking about this is a great idea," Molly agreed, sitting on the bed. "Talking you out of it would be even better."

"Spill it, Lowell, and make it good," Serena said.

Alex sighed. They had a point. Going through what had happened would clear her thoughts. As it was, the whole episode was a blur of excitement.

"Okay." She sat down cross-legged on the bed. "It all began with the pregnant concierge going into labor…"

A smile lifted Serena's lips. "You certainly know how to begin a story."

But Jayne wasn't smiling when the story ended. "Careful, sweetie. I smell heartbreak if you stay. Wyatt McKendrick looks like a man who's run through a lot of women. Rich, sophisticated women."

And Alex wasn't either rich or sophisticated.

"But he's offering you your dream, isn't he?" Molly asked. "The chance to open your shop sooner. That's the appeal, isn't it?"

"Partly," Alex said. "Without this chance I might never make enough money to open the shop. But it's more than that. All my life I've ended up in situations where I had no power and no stable home. After my father and my stepfather left, my mother struggled to support us. Sometimes we got evicted. We never had a real home. Later, there were men. Always temporary. Robert, the athlete I tutored, who left me for the prom queen; Leo, the painfully shy guy I mentored and turned into a woman-magnet only to have him slip away with someone he'd known all his life. Then Michael… He was struggling to be a single father. I was helping him. I thought we were going to make a home together, but we're not."

"Alex," Jayne said. "That's what worries me. I read somewhere that McKendrick's is competing for an award and…we know you so well. You're too darn warm-hearted. You jump in to help and end up getting hurt by men who don't appreciate what you've done for them."

"Which is exactly why I'm safe this time," Alex said. "Jayne, I'm aware of the mistakes I've made in the past. Those men I helped and fell in love with but who didn't love me back—they were my training ground. The scars I picked up will protect me, because now I know that if I want a home—and I do, more than anything—I'll have to make my own. From now on I'm declaring my independence from men who never offer forever or stability, anyway. I'm going after what I want, and when I get that shop I'm putting my whole heart in it. The money Wyatt is offering me could help speed up that process."

"What about your Web site?" Molly asked.

"I can update that from anywhere."

"You'll probably be living at the hotel. That won't be anything like a home. You know how you cling to that little apartment you've lived in for four years."

"I know, but I won't be here long."

"So you're staying?"

"I don't know. It's difficult. I'd miss all of you and… *wow*…this has happened so quickly that I'm not thinking straight. I do know that during those moments when I was manning the concierge desk it was exciting and…powerful. A little taste of what it'll be like running my own place. It was totally crazy, but I liked it."

"And then along came gorgeous Wyatt McKendrick, offering to let you have that power every single day," Serena suggested.

Alex and Serena studied each other. She knew that Serena was worried about the possibility of Wyatt hurting her if she stayed here without her friends as a buffer.

"If I stayed, it wouldn't have anything to do with Wyatt," she said. "I only spent a few minutes with him."

"So in those few minutes what did you think?" Molly asked.

"He runs a great hotel," Alex said. Good answer.

"How about those eyes? I love amber eyes," Serena said.

"But they're green." Alex frowned…and then groaned.

"Alex…" Jayne said, but Alex shook her head.

"If it makes you feel better, if I *do* decide to take this job, it won't be because Wyatt has gorgeous eyes."

"But I'll bet it doesn't hurt," Molly said sympathetically.

No, it didn't. And that might be a problem. If she stayed, she would have to keep a constant watch over her traitorous body and emotions. Fortunately she'd already been exposed to the dangers of making emotional mistakes. She was getting quite good at the recovery and moving on part, and she was determined to conquer the avoidance part, too. All she had to do was remember one thing: Wyatt was the kind of man who would break her heart without even being aware of it. So there could be *no* fantasizing about him. At all.

"Just…don't make this decision in haste," Jayne said.

"We wish you'd come home with us," Molly added.

A part of Alex agreed. Home was a known quantity. Her apartment was tiny, but unlike this job it wasn't temporary. Her real job offered no excitement but no dangers, either.

"I'll probably leave with you," Alex agreed.

Unless I don't, she thought. Inwardly, she sighed and started counting to ten. She kept counting until her urge to decide quickly, take the money and worry about the potential pitfalls later, subsided.

After dinner, Serena and Molly went out to a hotel bar, but Alex and Jayne chose an evening by one of the hotel's pools. Both of them wanted some quiet time, and the Amber Moon Pool, with its fragrant tropical landscaping, underwater amber lights, low-key background music and swinging hammocks was just the "escape to paradise" mood they wanted. The stress Jayne had been going through and the weekend's nonstop activity had left her exhausted. She needed to recharge her engine before finishing up tomorrow, and Alex just needed the relaxation of water.

"I need to think," Alex told her friends.

"You're supposed to be having fun," Serena reminded her.

Alex thought back to those adrenaline-charged minutes when she had controlled the lobby of McKendrick's and she smiled. "I *am* having fun," she said. Too much fun, maybe, but...

She knew then that she was going to say yes to Wyatt McKendrick's job offer. It probably wasn't that dangerous, anyway. He was, as Jayne had said, a man who probably had a lot of women, so he wouldn't be interested in her. She wouldn't be spending much time with him. At least outside of her daydreams.

Wyatt was surprised at his impatience to hear Alex's decision. He had hired and fired lots of people, always basing his decisions on what was best for the hotel. Firing someone was unpleasant. But hiring? Completely a cut-and-dried decision.

It's just the timing, he thought. He'd already been cutting things close, trying to locate someone of Belinda's caliber. Losing her so soon had caught him off-guard. So his mood had nothing to do with Alex's blue eyes or the curve of her mouth when she smiled.

But when he saw her crossing the lobby, in a poppy-red dress that showed off those amazing long legs, his gut tightened. His male antenna went on full alert. Too bad he was never going to do anything about that.

She smiled at him tentatively. If there was ever a look of "just let me get through this," Alex was wearing it.

Wyatt steeled himself for her *Thank you, but...* speech.

Instead, her smile grew as she drew closer. "So, what do we do first?" she asked. "If I'm going to do this, I want to be good at it."

A slow thrum of pleasure slid through his body. "You'll be good at it."

"You don't know that."

"Didn't we have this discussion yesterday? The one where you tried to convince me that you might be a criminal?"

"I did not. I merely implied that you didn't know anything about me." That pretty little nose lifted in the air. Somehow Wyatt kept from smiling.

"I think I might have mentioned that I intend to find out all about you. I may have seen your raw talent, but I assure you that I'm a very astute businessman."

"As if I didn't know that. I mean…look at this place, Mr. McKendrick."

"It's Wyatt. All my employees call me Wyatt."

She raised a brow. For half a second he thought she was going to give him a lecture on sound business practices. He half wished that she would, just for the entertainment value of it.

Instead she shook herself, as if forbidding herself to give that lecture. "Well, okay. Wyatt. But anyone can see that this place is a palace, and you're the man who keeps the lights lit. It's obvious that you know what you're doing."

"And you're worried that you won't know what *you're* doing?"

"If I leave my job to do this and things don't work out, I'll be worse off than I was before I said yes."

"Things will work out. I'll train you."

"If you do that, you might as well do the job yourself."

He arched an eyebrow.

"What?" she asked.

"I've never met anyone who tried so hard to convince me *not* to hire them."

"I just want to make sure we understand each other."

He looked into her eyes. "Okay, here's my part. I need a concierge and I've decided you're it. Barring a major miscalculation on my end, you'll slide into the job smoothly. Now, you tell me your part."

She stared right back. "I intend to be the best darn substitute concierge you've ever seen."

"Only the best *substitute*?"

She lifted one delicate shoulder in a shrug, an action that wasn't meant to be erotic but turned Wyatt hot. "Well, I didn't want to sound like I was dissing Belinda."

"I'm sure she'd appreciate that."

"How is she?"

"Mother of a baby girl named Misty."

"Oh, I *love* that name. I'll bet she's a sweetheart." The look of naked longing in Alex's eyes served as a warning to Wyatt. Alex could apparently make him burn just by lifting her shoulder an inch, but she was not a woman he could desire. She was the hearth and home type, and he'd never be that guy. He'd missed that imprinting process.

"Are you ready?" he asked.

"Yes. There's just one thing."

"And that is…"

"When the afternoon comes, my friends are leaving…"

"Friends. Of course."

He wasn't a man who cultivated friendships. Another failure to imprint, he supposed. Or…no. It was a choice. Letting people get close enabled them to see too much and gave them too much power. It left a person vulnerable, and he would never do anything that left him vulnerable again. Still, he understood the value of promoting the goodwill of employees.

"You'll want to see them off."

"They're my closest friends."

"Friends who are on vacation with you."

"Yes, but I made a deal with *you*."

"And I'll expect you to be on duty every day, beginning tomorrow. I demand punctuality and good attendance from my employees, but frankly you saved my rear, so I'm not inclined to make you cut your vacation short. We'll manage to scrape by one more day by having people do double duty and juggling a bit. Fortunately I have no meetings scheduled, and I'm capable of directing people around my own facility when necessary."

She frowned again. "Already I don't like the way this is starting. Your other employees will resent being asked to cover for me."

"My other employees know who signs their paychecks. They also know I'll compensate them for their trouble and that I'll return the favor when they need an emergency day off."

"I don't like to shirk my duties."

Wyatt gave her his most intimidating look—the one that had been known to make those on his payroll shake in their shoes. "We're not going to argue about this."

Alex looked completely unperturbed. "No, of course not. I'm totally aware that you're in charge, but still…"

Again he had that urge to smile, and Wyatt had never been a man given to smiles. Without missing a beat, he stepped over to a cabinet, opened a drawer, pulled out a handful of brochures and held them out to Alex.

"What's this?"

"Homework. If you're going to play hooky, I'll at least expect you to start educating yourself about the local attractions and the hotel."

The woman's smile could have lit the ballroom at

McKendrick's. The impact of it nearly sent Wyatt reeling. "I'll do that. Is there anything else?"

Yes. Stop smiling, he wanted to say. *Stop making me think of you as a woman I want to touch, and just be what you have to be, a very temporary employee.* "Yes, there is one thing."

She waited.

"Enjoy your day off."

"I will. And…thank you."

"For what?"

Her lips curved up more. "You're making it possible for me to fulfill my dreams."

Wyatt wanted to groan. He wished she hadn't said that. Dreamers were delicate creatures who could be easily hurt by men like him. He'd been a dreamer once, a long time ago. These days he gave the naive and the innocently optimistic a wide berth.

"Meet me here first thing tomorrow. I'll get you started."

Because the sooner he got her established, the sooner he could start thinking of her as just another employee.

He hoped.

CHAPTER FOUR

ALEX watched her friends pack their bags. Despite their plans to party up until the last minute, the day had been oddly subdued. The night before they'd each gone their separate ways, and this morning Serena had been distracted and flushed at breakfast.

"Yes, I had an...interesting evening," she'd said, but neglected to give any details.

"Very nice," was all Molly had said about her time the night before, but Alex had noticed that she'd glanced away.

And now that the time had come for them to part company, no one looked very cheerful. Jayne was even more beautiful with her new hairstyle, but the pain in her eyes was more intense than before the weekend had started. Still, she gave her friends a determined smile.

"This vacation was just what I needed," she said. "I'm glad you suggested it, Serena."

"It was an impulse," Serena said. "Maybe not my best." They all looked at Alex.

"I'm fine," she said. "When will I ever get an opportunity like this again? Besides, I'll be back in San Diego soon, living my dream, and we'll have a party to celebrate."

"A huge party," Molly agreed.

"The biggest and best," Serena added.

Then there was nothing left to say. The three of them had to leave or they'd miss their plane.

"Promise you'll stay in touch?" Molly gave Alex a hug.

"By phone, e-mail, text and every way possible," Alex agreed.

"And don't let that gorgeous hunk of a boss of yours work you too hard," Serena added.

All of them laughed at that. Alex thrived on hard work.

"I'll get plenty of downtime."

"And above all, don't…" Jayne hesitated. "He's too attractive to be safe, Alex."

"I won't fall in love with him, Jayne," Alex said solemnly. "Today several of the other employees have sidled up to me to tell me that every woman falls in love with him, but there's something mysterious about his past and he never gets involved with employees or falls in love, so I've been warned. Not that I needed to be. I've been burned too many times to ever fall for a man who comes with a 'guaranteed to break a girl's heart' tag sewn into his shirts." Love had only ever brought her pain, and now she was allergic. She was through with it.

Jayne managed a smile. She hugged Alex. "I would hate him so much if he hurt you."

"That won't happen. I'm not interested, and he's definitely not interested." Alex's words were as much a warning for herself as reassurance for her friends.

"Okay, but if you need us…for anything…" Serena began.

"We're only a few hours away," Molly added.

Then they all piled into a cab and were gone.

Alex was on her own. But tomorrow, and for a lot of tomorrows, she would be working for Wyatt McKendrick.

At last she let the full reality of that thought sink in, and admitted that she wasn't nearly as unaffected as she had told her friends. A sleepless night followed, only emphasizing the pitfalls of this situation. But when morning came there was no putting off the moment…or the man.

She had just signed on to work with the man dubbed the most elusive bachelor in Las Vegas. And unfortunately she *did* find him attractive, and she *was* nervous.

But she had never been one to stand meekly by awaiting her fate. She tended to plow forcefully ahead…just the way her unlucky-in-love mother had done.

And that, of course, was the problem. But it was one she intended to rectify.

"So, let's get this thing done, Wyatt McKendrick," she muttered. Because the sooner he gave her some direction, the sooner she could go about her business, away from any danger of getting too close to the man.

"I'm ready," Alex said, as she met Wyatt coming out of his office. "Where do I begin?"

He raised a brow. "I'm glad you're so enthusiastic. You argued vociferously against taking this job."

"But now I have, and I intend to jump in with both feet."

Which brought his gaze to her feet and her open-toed low-heeled sandals…which made Alex aware of her feet in a way she never had been before. She felt a bit exposed. But she couldn't let him see that, so she thrust her chin up and waited.

"Okay," he agreed. "But technically you're not due at your desk for another hour, so I've made arrangements to introduce you to some of the people I prefer to refer customers to."

"Such as…"

"Travel agents, tour guides, other business contacts."

She pulled a small blue notepad out of her purse. "All right, I'm ready."

A trace of a smile lifted his lips. He reached out and plucked the notepad from her grasp. "There's a fact sheet with everyone's contact information on it at your desk. The purpose of this outing is for me to introduce you and for you to inhale the details of the businesses you'll be referring customers to. I want you to note what makes these businesses the best that can be had even if the customer never enters their premises. I've worked with some of them for the entire time I've been here."

"You're not native to Las Vegas?"

"No. A transplant from a small town in Illinois. I came here five years ago, not knowing a soul, but Las Vegas fits me."

She tilted her head and studied him. "Wow, you stayed even though you had no friends or family here? That's intriguing. So many people fly into Las Vegas for a weekend or a week."

"And most of them leave," he said, finishing her thoughts. "But they come to have fun. I came because a person can start from square one here and make things happen quickly."

Alex looked up at the high atrium ceiling of the lobby. The room was green and gold, with light streaming in and turning everything molten. With its creamy marble floors and subtle gold offsets, the whole atmosphere was one of richness. But Alex knew from her weekend here that the magic began beyond this lobby. The hotel was divided into two wings. One was focused on pampering oneself with meditation and relaxation and places for private meetings or total solitude, the other was set up for treating oneself to life's beaches and parties. Both, however, echoed the richness of this room.

"Did you design this place yourself?" she asked.

"Most of it."

"You did an outstanding job. My friends and I came here because Jayne was jilted. We needed some escapism. McKendrick's is the perfect escape."

"Thank you. It's a work in progress."

"You're changing things?" She'd spent too much of her life watching things change and slip away. Or maybe *things* was the wrong word. She'd watched *people* change and she'd paid the price.

"You don't approve?"

"The hotel is perfect as it is."

"Perfection—or imperfection—is a matter of opinion, isn't it?"

Alex studied him. His tone had been light, but for a second she'd seen a hint of something *not* light in his eyes.

"Has someone been criticizing McKendrick's?" she asked.

He looked amused. "You sound defensive."

"Hey, I work at McKendrick's," she teased. "I've been here for—" she glanced at her watch "—five whole minutes, and I'll have you know that I'm intensely loyal."

Also prone to immersing herself in situations, she reminded herself. Was she really already lecturing her boss? Getting too involved? That would definitely have to stop.

"I'm glad to know that. But change can be good," he said. "If McKendrick's is to stay at the top of the game I have to keep making it better."

She nodded. "Belinda said something about it being awards season?"

"Yes," he answered, his green eyes intense. "McKendrick's has been nominated for one of the more prestigious ones, but the competition is fierce and there's no guarantee of success. I rely on my employees who deal with the customers to note ways we can improve, so don't be shy."

Alex chuckled.

"What?" Wyatt asked.

"No one would ever say that I'm shy about offering my opinions. Too often I can't keep my mouth shut."

His gaze lowered to Alex's mouth, and she suddenly felt short of breath. He slowly shook his head. "I wouldn't worry about your mouth…as long as you're being helpful. I'm a demanding employer, but I don't pass judgment unless a crime has been committed. You can speak freely to me."

That was heady and possibly dangerous territory. She had a reputation for being overzealous about fixing things. She tried too hard. And often, if people weren't overwhelmed by her, they took advantage. She gave too much. They took too much. But those had been nonwork situations, and Wyatt *was* her boss. Somehow that was both freeing and frightening. He was out of her league and she was in over her head.

But she didn't have much time to think about that. Within minutes Wyatt had handed her into his sleek black sports car, and her education had begun.

The businesses Wyatt took her to were all opulent, the owners gracious. They took the time to explain what she could call on them for and to assure her that she could expect their help if she was uncertain of what a customer needed, but what struck her even more was the respectful but formal relationship each of them seemed to have with Wyatt. There was no friendly banter of the type she enjoyed with *her* business associates. They clearly admired Wyatt, but he maintained a distance.

"Thank you, Harold. Alex and I will be in touch," he told the owner of Barrington Tours.

The man nodded. "I'm very pleased to meet you, Alex," he said, his tone warm. "Call on me if you have any questions."

"You might regret that," she teased. "I tend to ask a lot of questions."

The man grinned. "Try me. I'll look forward to it. Really."

When she'd thanked him and turned to leave, she noticed Wyatt standing with his arms crossed, watching the exchange, a slightly disapproving look in his eyes. She was tempted to look down at herself to see if her bra strap was showing. Instead, she smiled. Others might be intimidated by Wyatt's height and stern looks, and her pulse might gallop at the sheer virility of the man, but none of that would ultimately matter. She was temporary. There couldn't be any danger here. She wouldn't allow it.

"Next?" she said with a bright smile.

"Last stop," Wyatt said as he drove her to the third shop. "Then I'll return you to your desk and let you get acclimated."

Alex nodded. She was expecting this stop to be like the last two, both of which had evidenced cool distance between Wyatt and the owners. Men respecting men, each carving out his own stoic space.

But when they entered an upscale clothing store, several female employees stopped to stare at Wyatt with naked longing in their eyes.

"Hello, Beverly, this is Alex, my new concierge," he said to a beautiful woman of indeterminate years. "She may be calling on you now and then. Beverly can provide a suit, dress shirt and tie in record time," he told Alex.

"Yes. I prefer *un*dressing men, but I'm an expert at dressing them," Beverly told Alex with a smile.

Alex liked the woman immediately. "Does it happen often?"

"Dressing or undressing?"

"Both," Alex said, refusing to blush. If she was going to work with this woman she needed to know how to hold her own.

Beverly laughed. "I like her," she told Wyatt, ignoring the fact that he was still maintaining his distance. "And, for the record, we almost never get to undress them—especially not the good-looking ones, like Wyatt. But you'd be amazed at how many men show up with too few shirts and then spill mustard on the one they need. And of course they go running to the closest concierge. You and I, we're going to be a team."

"I'll put you on my speed dial," Alex said. "I'll memorize your number."

"Oh, you're good. We're going to have fun. Wyatt, you be good to her and don't scare her away with those forbidding stares of yours. Don't make her fall in love with you, either. It's the surest way to lose a good employee."

Alex blanched. "That won't be a problem. I've sworn off men."

Beverly snorted. "Honey, we *all* swear off men now and then. But when someone like Wyatt comes along, we forget what we promised not to do."

Alex wanted to glance at Wyatt, to see his expression. He had been silent during this whole exchange. He hadn't admonished Beverly, but he hadn't responded, either. She remembered the warning about employees falling in love with him. "I won't forget," she told Beverly.

"Beverly, stop badgering Alex," Wyatt finally said. "That's not why I brought her here, and she's not interested."

Beverly wrinkled her nose. "That's what I say about chocolate. Every single morning. And don't you try to intimidate me with those frowns, Wyatt. It might work with everyone else, but not with me."

Almost despite himself, it seemed, Wyatt smiled. He said goodbye, Alex bade Beverly farewell, and they both wandered out into the sunlight. "I'm sorry about that," he said.

"Don't be. I like people who speak their minds. And I definitely like having all the cards on the table."

He nodded. "As in admitting that you've sworn off men?"

"I mean it. You don't have to worry."

"I wasn't, and it was worth knowing. I don't intrude on my employees' private lives, but I do try to protect them when I can. It's safe to assume that being one of the public faces of McKendrick's and an attractive woman, there'll be men who'll try to hit on you. I assume you ran into some jerks in the past. If you should ever feel pressured by a customer and need assistance, Randy or I will deal with them."

Alex shook her head. "I'm able to take care of myself, and I wouldn't say that my attitude about men has anything to do with the ones I knew being jerks. I just ran into some hard truths about myself. I'm a woman who leaps when other people walk, and I also like to stay in one place when the men that I've known are changing and rushing off to something new. I want a home, stability, a fulfilling career and maybe children."

"But you agreed to work here when you wanted to stay in San Diego?"

"Only because you bribed me."

He held out his hands in surrender. "I did, didn't I?"

"Blatantly."

"I'm not apologizing."

"I'm not asking you to. Working here gets me that much closer to where I want to be. It's short-term, and in the end I'll go back to what I love, anyway."

"And maybe someday you'll meet the right kind of man."

"Unlikely. I'm happy doing what I'm doing, and giving up men is kind of freeing. I can totally concentrate on my long-term goals—the things I've been waiting for and wanting."

"Goals are good."

"Spoken like a true businessman. Do *you* have others? Besides McKendrick's, I mean." The words had just popped out. "Forget I said that," she said. "As my boss, your goals are totally none of my business."

He shrugged. "The truth? I'm strictly business when it comes to goals. In two months it'll be five years since I bought McKendrick's. I want to expand the business and send it to everyone's top ten list of hotels. So no personal goals, if that's what you were asking. I learned long ago that I'm not suited to relationships, but that's a boring story and we have to get back. I want you to have a little downtime so that you're completely comfortable when you take your place behind the desk."

But Alex had a feeling that she was never going to be entirely comfortable at McKendrick's. Her job was the hotel, and Wyatt and the hotel were intimately entwined. No matter how she looked at things, she'd be spending a lot of time with him.

Just as an employee, she reminded herself. She thought the words, her brain registered them, but heaven help her, when she looked at Wyatt she didn't feel even slightly "comfortable." She felt…hot.

What a totally alarming thought. If she hadn't been committed to work, she would have been calling up Jayne, Serena and Molly right then, and asking them to talk her down off the ledge. As it was…

"I'm yours for the day, Wyatt," she said. A totally cringeworthy statement, but one that was, in fact, true.

She had committed herself to Wyatt, not just for a day but for weeks to come. She might as well accept that and arm herself heavily against her unwanted blatantly physical reaction to the man. Beverly was right about one thing. The man was too much like chocolate. Tempting. He definitely threatened her "no men" diet.

All the way back to the hotel, Wyatt wondered what in hell he was doing. There was training an employee, and then there was enjoying oneself with an employee. The second wasn't allowed. He needed his walls.

So, despite the fact that he had enjoyed watching Alex's exchange with Beverly, he was also glad that Alex's questions had forced him to remember not only his goals but his past, his flaws, his limitations. He'd been born not fitting with other people—from his mother, who'd given birth to him and then dumped him on relatives, to those relatives who'd tried to beat the wildness out of him, to the women who had wanted him and been disappointed when he disappointed *them*. All of his relationships had left someone with scars, and he was through with them.

In that sense, working with Alex might present a minefield. She seemed both tough and fragile, like a woman who needed a knight in shining armor but didn't know it. What she didn't need was a loner who would break her heart again. What *he* didn't need was to break someone's heart or fail to live up to expectations again. He didn't have to be reminded that some people started out bad and tough and stayed that way. McKendrick's was the only place where he excelled, and he needed to remember that.

Hiring Alex might be good for McKendrick's, but bad for him. Except she was on a break from men and he was on a permanent break from relationships. So maybe this employer/employee relationship *could* work, he thought as he drove down the road. He hoped so.

Though he didn't broadcast the details, his need for

McKendrick's to succeed ran deep. It was almost fifteen years since he had escaped his hellish home and the people who had beaten him down and predicted that he would never amount to anything. He was finally up, higher than anyone had ever expected him to be. This hotel was where his life had truly begun. It was his validation and his legacy.

Everything else had to be secondary, and he couldn't forget that. If he did, someone might get hurt.

CHAPTER FIVE

ALEX didn't have any more time to think about Wyatt, because as soon as she got to her desk, a man came up wanting to know the best place for a haircut. *Don't panic. Don't tell him you don't have a clue, or remember that this hotel is up for an award and reviewers might be anonymous men asking about haircuts.*

She glanced around the room. Hmm, Randy's haircut was nice, but probably not what the fiftyish man was looking for. She scanned the room further, saw what she was looking for, then waved to Randy.

He frowned, but came over. "Randy, could you watch my desk for just a second?"

He blinked. The man who had asked the question blinked.

"I'll be right back with your answer," she said, striding across the lobby toward a waiter who was serving drinks to two women seated next to a fountain. As the man turned from his task, Alex flashed a smile. "Hi, I'm Alex Lowell, the new concierge, Seth," she said, reading off his name tag. "When you're done, I have a quick question."

He nodded as she turned to the women and held out her hand. "Hello, and welcome to McKendrick's. If you need anything at all, I hope you'll let me know."

"Actually, I *do* need something," one woman said. "I have

to know...where did you get that fantastic outfit?" She gestured toward Alex's pale lemon knee-length suit.

Alex grimaced inside. She wanted to be helpful, and yet... "I'm afraid I got it in San Diego."

"Wonderful! I've been wanting to go there. Now I can schedule a shopping trip as an excuse. I have a luncheon in a month, and that's just what I was looking for. You wouldn't happen to have the address of the shop, would you?"

"As a matter of fact, I do," Alex said, writing down the information for her friend's shop. "Tell Elaine, the owner, that Alexandra Lowell sent you. She'll treat you right."

"Fantastic! Now, I better let you get to Seth. He's certainly in demand this morning."

Alex smiled. "Yes. Seth, I need the name of your hairdresser? Barber? Whoever gave you that great cut?"

Seth blinked.

"It's for a customer," she explained. "You have just the right look, I think."

The women agreed that Seth had great hair, and chuckled as he blushed and smiled and scribbled an address down.

"Thanks, Seth. You're a lifesaver. I'm sure Mr. Toliver will thank you, too." She flashed the women a smile. "I hope you find something nice at Elaine's."

"Even if I don't, I'll enjoy looking. It was great meeting someone who takes her job personally. By the way, Alex, I'm Joanne. Wyatt runs a great hotel, and even though we're local, Meredith and I come here often, so it's good to meet you."

"Thank you. I'll do my best to make your stay special."

Then, because Mr. Toliver had been waiting too long, Alex practically flew across the room.

"I'm sorry I took so long, Mr. Toliver. Thank you, Randy. I was just getting some expert advice on hairstylists from Seth."

"Alex," Randy said in a low voice, "Seth is a waiter."

"Yes, and he has gorgeous hair, doesn't he? Both of those ladies love it, too. I think you'll be in good hands at—" she glanced at the piece of paper "—Gregory's, Mr. Toliver. If women as stylish as Joanne and Meredith admire Seth's hair, that's a stellar recommendation."

Mr. Toliver glanced toward the middle-aged attractive women. One of them smiled at him. "Well, Gregory's it is, then," he said. "Thank you, young lady."

"It was a pleasure. Come back if you need anything else."

When the man had gone, Randy shook his head. "You're supposed to look in the files. We have lists of places you can recommend."

"But I don't know anything about those places."

"Alex, you were lucky this time. Frank Toliver is a frequent and valued customer here, but he could have been anybody. McKendrick's is having its fifth anniversary, so it's in the crosshairs of every reviewer, most of whom work incognito. Not only that, but this is the first time that the hotel is a finalist for a National Travel Award. We're up against some fierce competition, including Champagne just down the road, so we have to be careful and make sure that every customer goes away satisfied. Most of our clients won't want to pattern themselves after people like Seth."

Alex felt a twinge. Was Randy right? Had she hit a wrong note in her first few minutes on the job?

"Seth the waiter?"

The deep voice came from behind Alex. She didn't have to turn around to know who it was, but she did. Time to face the music. Maybe it really *had* been a mistake not to fly back to San Diego with her friends.

To his credit, Randy merely looked sheepish and didn't try

to discredit her. Alex opened her mouth, wondering if she should apologize, and yet…

"I like Seth's hair," she said. "But I really didn't even think about the fact that Mr. Toliver might not want to frequent the same establishments that our employees do. Actually, I don't even *know* what kind of neighborhood I sent him to."

And she didn't have the address on her any longer, either.

"I'm sure Seth wouldn't have led a customer into a dark alley," Wyatt assured her. "So…you like Seth's hair, do you?"

She pushed her chin up. "I do."

He frowned. "I'm not criticizing, Alex. I'm just waiting."

"For what?"

"To see what Frank Toliver looks like when he gets back, and to see how he feels about how he looks. If it goes well, we'll add Gregory's to our list of recommended shops."

Alex couldn't help wondering what Mr. Toliver would do or say if he *didn't* like how he looked. Would it affect his opinion of McKendrick's service?

She could tell Randy was thinking the same thing. He was practically leaning over, listening to see if Wyatt was going to say more.

Wyatt frowned at him. "The desk," he said. That was all. Randy left for his post and the customers headed that way.

"I suppose I should stick to what Belinda has on her list," Alex said. "Winging it might not be the best idea until I know more about the city and the best places to go."

"You saw a need. You took care of it. That's why I hired you, Alex," Wyatt said. "Every customer is important, but our reputation won't rise or fall on one customer's opinion. If, by some chance, Frank Toliver is less than happy with your recommendation, then I'll take care of the situation. He'll be given a few extras courtesy of the hotel. By the time he leaves, he'll be pampered and smiling."

"And you'll have had extra work because of me."

"That's my call to make."

"But you didn't hire me so that you could clean up my messes. If I'm to be useful, I have to get things right."

That was, Alex thought, a version of what she had told herself as a child, and later as an adult. If she just did things right, her father would come home, her stepfather would visit her, Robert or Leo or Michael would be blown away by what a difference she'd made in their lives. She hated the fact that she'd even remembered that right now, but at least this time her concern wasn't about winning love. It was about the job she'd been hired to do and about the National Travel Awards. As a finalist in the competition, the hotel was under the microscope, and she intended to help it shine.

"I hired you to help the customers, Alex. I'm the only one who gets to decide how you're progressing."

The only one. He really was a lone wolf—the nickname she'd heard him called. Alex couldn't help thinking that she had spent her life wanting companionship while Wyatt appeared to wrap himself in his solitary status.

"You heard Randy criticize me. I hope you won't hold it against him. He was just trying to give me good advice."

"Randy sometimes gets carried away, but as I said earlier he's good at what he does."

"I see that," Alex said, watching Randy smile at a woman who appeared to be complaining loudly about something. The woman's voice rose, but Randy kept his expression calm, the low tones of his response soothing, until finally the woman nodded and walked away. "I fully intend to get along with Randy. Maybe I'll ask him for some suggestions."

"I'm sure he'd like that. But remember what I said. I hired you because of your ability to take control of a situation and connect with the patrons. A minor mistake or two won't topple McKendrick's."

Maybe not, but Alex had tangled others up in her mistakes more than once. While she'd been fooling herself into thinking shy Leo would fall in love with her, the heart of the equally shy girl who'd loved him from afar for years had been breaking. Far worse than that, though, was what she'd inadvertently done to little Mia. Assuming that she and her most recent ex, Michael, had a future, she'd allowed herself to get close to Michael's daughter, and the child had been heartbroken when things had fallen apart. The fact that she'd harmed a child in much the same way she had been harmed, scalded her. It was something she couldn't forgive herself for. It was a reminder that there was a high price for some mistakes.

"Randy says you're competing against another Las Vegas hotel for the award."

He maintained an expression that told her nothing. "Champagne will be tough to beat. They'll keep upping the ante right until the end."

So the competition *was* a big deal. "What are the odds that you'll win?"

"Winning isn't guaranteed," Wyatt said, his tone cool. But she could tell by the way his jaw tightened that the award meant something to him.

And why not? He'd designed the hotel himself. That made the award important, whether he wanted to admit it or not. It seemed he didn't want to admit it to *her*. And why should he? She was an employee. A stranger.

"You're the boss," she said. "I'll do my best to be as mistake-free as possible while I get acclimated."

"I'm not anticipating lots of mistakes."

She shrugged. "Neither am I, but everyone makes them. I've made my share."

"Are we talking about the film crew and the CPR incident?"

"Among other things."

Wyatt raised an eyebrow. "I'll keep that in mind."

"That I might go through some rough patches the first few days?"

He studied her, his expression unreadable. "That you know CPR. And that you didn't hesitate to help." He held her gaze to make his point. There was something fierce and commanding about the man. Heat seemed to radiate off him, despite the fact that he seemed so outwardly cool.

Disregarding her warnings to behave, Alex's heart-rate sped up. Warmth spread through her. She tried to ignore it, even though the man had eyes that could make a woman forget to be smart. "Well…" Somehow she managed to find her voice. "As embarrassing as it was, I'd do it again. But for now I'd better start learning the ropes if we're going to win that award. I'll just read the reference material that Randy tells me is in the cabinets, and surf the Internet for interesting factoids about Las Vegas."

"Wyatt, there you are! I've been looking everywhere."

The husky female voice came from Alex's right, and she turned to see a gorgeous blonde woman moving toward them. She wore a sand-colored sheath dress that fit her perfectly. Her bare legs and arms were smoothly toned and tanned, and her megawatt smile was focused on Wyatt.

Alex instinctively took a step back. The woman knew Wyatt, and Wyatt was Alex's boss, not her friend.

Wyatt, however, drew her forward. "Katrina, this is Alexandra, my new concierge. Alex, Katrina owns Gendarmes, a restaurant down the street."

"Ah, one of your colleagues," Alex said with a smile.

The woman's smile dimmed. "Oh, yes," she said, her tone clear. Alex didn't rank. "We both have a shared interest in Las Vegas and…other things. Come on, Wyatt, we're going to be late."

A frown line appeared between his brows. "Alex, I'll be at a meeting of some of the local hoteliers and restaurants most of the rest of the day. We're coordinating some functions and we'll be at Gendarmes, but if there's an emergency I can be interrupted."

Alex almost thought she heard Katrina hiss.

"Thank you, but I'm not expecting any emergencies," Alex said.

Still, after the two of them had gone Alex admitted that she'd felt the telling sting of jealousy when Katrina had walked away with Wyatt at her side. Allowing herself to feel that way *would* rank as an emergency. Not to mention how incredibly stupid it would be. Developing an infatuation for one's boss was such a cliché and just…wrong. Besides, while she'd pursued love with reckless abandon and lost before, she'd at least had good reason to expect success in those cases. Wyatt McKendrick was a sure ticket to heartbreak. She just couldn't allow herself to fall for someone incapable of loving her. Never again.

Love, Alex had discovered, was a lethal weapon in the hands of the wrong person. *She* was the wrong person and always had been. Her current dreams were within reach, and she wouldn't cheapen them by setting them aside to covet the impossible. Fantasizing about Wyatt wasn't allowed, and she was just going to have to nip that trip to Jealous Town in the bud.

So she devoted herself to learning the ropes. She read everything on the desk, thumbing through pamphlets and cruising Internet travel sites. She answered basic questions, made reservations for people and directed them to where they wanted to go. In a slow moment she wandered over to Randy's desk and picked his brain.

He looked at her suspiciously, but then told her what she needed to know. "You're really throwing yourself into this, aren't you?" he asked.

"I agreed to take the job. I'm going to do it right."

"Could I give you a word of advice?"

"Yes."

"Don't do it to please Wyatt. Women always fall in love with him, but he's a guy who likes his personal space. He doesn't get close to anyone, male or female. And while he occasionally escorts a woman for both business and…other obvious reasons, he doesn't stay."

"Grr."

"Don't tell me you've already fallen?"

"No, but you must be the tenth person who's told me that. So, for the tenth time, I'm never going to fall in love with Wyatt. I'm safe."

"You say that as if you're trying to convince yourself, but I've seen it happen before."

"I'll be fine."

"Good. But if the unexpected should happen and your 'never ever' turns to 'maybe', will *Wyatt* be fine?"

She blinked.

"Look, none of us know Wyatt that well. He keeps his personal life to himself. But he treats his employees well, even if he asks a lot in return. I know that better than anyone. I'm here today because Wyatt caught me trying to pick his pocket when my mother died and left me and my younger brother destitute. He grabbed me by my shirt, lectured me, and then gave me a job with the understanding that I would keep out of trouble. Because he's fair, those of us who work for him pay attention, and what we've seen is that he takes everything that concerns McKendrick's seriously. If he chose you to work here and you somehow got hurt, he would brood over that.

"The truth is that whenever a woman shows up here with stars in her eyes, and he has to tell her no, he retreats into himself even more than usual. His past's a secret, but something must have happened, because even if he'd never admit it, hurting people seems to affect him almost as much as it does them. Unless they deserve it, of course. Then he can be ruthless."

"So you want me to protect Wyatt's psyche by agreeing not to fall in love with him?"

"It sounds stupid, but, yes, something like that."

"Not a problem. You've got it." She hoped her voice didn't wobble with uncertainty when she said that.

"Good, because people are already taking bets on how long it will be before you go down for the count."

"Randy!"

"I'm just saying…"

"Well, stop saying. I'm here to do a good job. That's all."

With that, Alex returned to her desk, more prepared than ever to keep a safe distance from Wyatt. And that meant concentrating harder on her job.

She dug out more of the guides from Belinda's desk and began to study them. She had to. Unlike someone who'd lived in the city, she didn't know anything about the layout other than the world famous Las Vegas Strip. That would have to change, something that became clear when several people asked her questions she didn't know the answers to. Fortunately they were nice enough to wait while she quizzed Randy. But Randy had his own duties, and her stalling techniques wouldn't bode well for McKendrick's if a reviewer for the competition showed up.

For two seconds Alex allowed self-doubt to creep in, but she battled it back. She had the ability to do this job, didn't she? Or if she didn't have it yet, she would. Knowledge was king in this position, but there had to be a better way to educate herself than sitting around reading tour guides. As soon as she got off work she planned to do her homework. The Alex way.

But for now…

"The elevators to the karaoke bar are that way," she told one young man, and, "The shuttle to the airport will be here in ten minutes," she told another.

She was searching through a drawer she hadn't had time to explore yet when she looked up and saw Mr. Toliver coming in through the main doors. Automatically she glanced up at his hair, which…mostly wasn't there.

Okay, this is so not what I expected, she thought. His hair looked nothing like Seth's sweeping blond mane. Still, *she* had sent him to the stylist; it was only right to follow up.

"Mr. Toliver," she called.

To her surprise, he smiled and turned her way. "What do you think?" he asked.

"I think…"

"It's short, I know," he said, rubbing his hand over the top of his head. "But Gregory told me that my head was shaped perfectly for the almost shaved look, and since I was starting to thin on the top I thought I'd try it. It's not for everybody, of course, but it's very freeing," he said, smiling. "Much cooler in this heat, too."

Alex sent a silent thank-you to Gregory, the hairdresser she'd never met. It seemed that McKendrick's had a happy customer. And the style *did* suit the man. "It looks right on you," she said. "Awesome."

He walked away, his smile even broader, and Alex followed his progress. Her gaze snagged on Wyatt, who had entered the building while she hadn't been watching. He was staring at Mr. Toliver, who had his back turned toward Wyatt.

Almost without thinking she stood up and moved toward the door. "It might look a little drastic," she began, "but—"

"He likes it. I know. I ran into him outside," Wyatt said. "Nice job." Something close to pleasure lurked in his green eyes and sent her heartbeat racing ten times faster than it had when she'd seen Frank Toliver's bald head.

Don't even consider wondering what he would look like if he ever flashed a full smile, she ordered herself. "Weren't you even a little worried when you saw his head?"

He hesitated, as if studying the question. "I already had my fingers poised over my cellphone to order champagne shipped to his room."

He sounded so disgruntled at even having to admit it that Alex couldn't hold back a small chuckle. "Aha, so you *were* worried."

Now the smallest trace of a smile lifted his lips. "If it makes you feel better, I *did* feel a twinge, but only a small one. Alex, in this business there are bound to be customers who have concerns now and then, but I hire good people. I expect them to do their jobs well, but in the end, I'm always poised to fix a few things. I'm the safety net. If you're doing everything possible to give the customers the experience they have every right to expect, you're doing what I require of you. Do we have a deal?"

He held out his hand. She stared at it, almost afraid to touch him.

And when she finally did place her hand in his, she knew

that she had been right to be afraid. The heat and the energy and the sudden attraction whooshed in, making it hard to forget that Wyatt was a man who was impossible to ignore.

A loner of a man, she reminded herself. His words just then had confirmed it as much as anything Randy had told her. He was an island—or at least he was the lone protector of the personal island that this hotel represented.

He was waiting for her answer. "We have a deal," she managed to choke out, but when he released her it was all she could do not to stare at her hand. It felt as if he had imprinted a part of himself on her.

"You're free to go, Alex," he said.

She frowned, confused.

"Lois is here for her shift," he clarified. "You've survived your first full day."

I'm not so sure, she thought as she walked away. She kept trying to tell herself that this was just a job, but her reaction to Wyatt made it feel more like a personal test.

Alex stared at her hand when she got back to her room. Sensation rushed through her, which was ridiculous. The man had merely shaken her hand, a brief brush of flesh against flesh, but the nerve-endings in her fingers had practically sizzled.

She was far too attracted to him, acting just the way Randy had predicted. Like an idiotic woman obsessed with Wyatt. Like those other women who had wanted him.

But she had one advantage over those women. She didn't *want* to want him. He was the most potent and unattainable man she'd ever met, and darn it, she wasn't going to do something stupid.

Alex took deep calming breaths. She counted to ten. "I'm strong. I'm not a slave to my emotions."

Those words were important because, like it or not, she was

once again in a position of helping a man achieve his goals, the very thing that had caused her to walk straight into heartbreak after heartbreak. Assisting a man created a rush of very temporary positive emotions, but when those emotions faded the party was over. The pain began.

Not happening this time, Lowell. Wyatt's goals were part of her job, nothing more. When she was done she could run back to San Diego, set up her shop, and enjoy the rest of her life.

"I can be attracted to you without succumbing, Wyatt," she whispered. "You won't have anything to regret when I'm gone. In fact, you're going to be glad you hired me, because I intend to help you surpass any competitors and win that prize."

And she knew just how she was going to start.

CHAPTER SIX

WYATT prowled the halls of McKendrick's, trying to shake off the feeling that he shouldn't have shaken Alex's hand. Ridiculous. He'd merely been trying to reassure her that she didn't have to bear the responsibility for the success of the hotel. He hadn't hired her for that.

What did you hire her for? he asked himself. Easy answer. He'd simply wanted a smooth transition between Belinda leaving and returning. Alex had seemed like a woman who could make that transition invisible for the customers and staff.

Unfortunately, she wasn't invisible to *him*—a fact he'd noticed from the minute he'd set eyes on her. The second she'd put her hand in his energy and desire had zipped up his arm, practically consuming him.

Then don't touch her again, he told himself. He didn't intend to. But how he wanted to.

It was a new day, one that had so far gone smoothly. Alex hadn't sent anyone to unknown locales. Nor had she followed her instincts and upbraided a man who had been loudly berating his wife about some nitpicky thing she had forgotten to do.

On the other hand she might have done that...if Wyatt hadn't appeared. He had clamped one hand on the man's shoulder and firmly if not gently shepherded the man to the side. Wyatt's eyes had brooked no argument, his voice had been commanding, but he had given the man an out, casually drawing him into conversation about how vexing travel could be. When the story of a plane stranded on the tarmac for hours had spilled out, Wyatt had relented, called for a bellboy to deliver the couple's luggage to their room and presented them with complimentary tickets to the spa for massages.

As they moved away, Alex could hear the man apologizing to his wife. "Nice," she said to Wyatt. "But the man looked as if he would explode when you pulled him aside. How did you know he wouldn't take your interference out on his wife?"

Wyatt stood very still, that cool stare trapping Alex in his sights. "You disapprove of my tactics, Alex?"

Alex was sure that she was blushing. "On the contrary. I'm glad that you took him aside and defused the situation. But...I was afraid he was going to hit you."

Wyatt shook his head. "He wasn't the type. I know the type."

The way he said that...as if he'd met men who'd used their fists on him...

She remembered what Randy had said about not knowing much about Wyatt. She should keep that in mind. A woman who couldn't handle men she knew well should definitely not tangle with men who were mysterious. Or dark. Or dangerous.

Slowly, so that he couldn't see how he affected her, she took a deep breath. "I'd better get back to work."

He tilted his head in acquiescence. "You should know that a few customers have complimented me on your helpfulness, and..."

"And?" She waited.

"And on your smile," he said, as if he hadn't really intended to admit that.

But his comment warmed her and emboldened her. "It never hurts to smile," she said. "Even if you're a McKendrick." Because he didn't smile. Not much.

And yet he looked amused. His eyes lost some of that fierceness. "I'll keep that in mind," he said. "Maybe I'll even write it down on a blue notepad."

Then he walked away. Had Wyatt McKendrick, he who kept his distance from his employees, just teased her?

He had. And that sent a tingle in a zipping, swirling course down her body.

Don't be affected, she told herself. But she found herself looking for him when her day ended. Which made her angry. Whether the anger was because she was looking for the man, or because she was unsuccessful in her quest, maybe even wondering if he was with the pretty restaurateur, she didn't want to know.

Besides, she had things to do. Last night she'd hit the town with a digital camera and her notepad, scoping out sights for a time when a customer might need help. But, being unfamiliar with the territory, she had covered very little ground. Tonight she would cover more.

Wyatt was on his way to his penthouse apartment late in the day when he turned a corner and nearly ran over Alex. She'd been walking while looking at a map and she bumped up against him, the map crumpling and tearing.

Instantly he caught her, stopping her forward momentum, heat branding him as his palms closed around the bare skin of her upper arms. Fragrant skin. Smooth skin.

Stop it, he ordered himself, glancing down. She was looking a bit dazed.

"I'm so sorry," she said. "I wasn't even looking where I was going." For two seconds they stood there, connected, as Wyatt tried to ignore how she felt…and how she looked, with those big, startled blue eyes.

Then reality kicked in and she took a step backward, gathering the crumpled, crinkling paper and trying to smooth it into something resembling a map again as he released her.

Walk away, he told himself. Treat this situation the way you would with any other employee.

But Alex wasn't like any other employee he'd ever hired. There was something about her that was difficult to ignore. Which was unfortunate. Ignoring people, not letting them get to him, was what enabled him to be who he was. It was how he had managed to survive a brutal childhood.

"Do you need directions?" he asked, ignoring his own good advice.

She smiled, that brilliant, room-brightening smile that his customers seemed to warm to. "I'm just having a little trouble figuring out where to start."

"Start?"

"Memorizing the city. I realized that if I'm going to be effective I need to know Las Vegas almost as well as I know San Diego. I have to be able to envision a place when someone asks me a question, so I'm trying to experience as much of the city as I can. Last night was easy. A cabdriver took me past a few of the popular restaurants for a survey of what's available. But what I really want is to totally lose myself in the whole Las Vegas scene. I thought I'd walk this time and surround myself with the city, but I'm having trouble deciding where to begin."

"Alexandra, you don't have to put in extra hours." He expected loyalty from his employees, but not servitude. He was the last man who would ever ask for that.

She frowned. "I'm not asking you to pay me for this. It's something I need to do for me. Tomorrow will be my third day on the job, and I'm determined to close the gaps in my knowledge."

"You're doing a good job."

She tilted her head. "Thank you. I'm not doubting myself. The past two days *have* been good. I'm starting to feel more settled. I just want to push myself a little harder, learn more. I have goals. By the end of this week I intend to be a winner at the 'totally invisible concierge' game." She gave him a dazzling conspiratorial smile that made his pulse leap.

Wyatt didn't have the heart to tell her that she was never going to be invisible. She was too darned electric, attractive, alive. But he knew what she meant. She didn't want anyone to be able to notice that she was still learning her job, so here she was with her map and her determination. And, yes, her good idea. Well, *almost* a good idea.

"I applaud your dedication," he said, "but wandering the streets alone with your head buried in a map? I don't think so."

Her chin lifted slightly. "I'm fully capable of taking care of myself. I know self-defense, and I have hairspray, a lighter and sharp keys in my purse."

"And if you're distracted, you'll never even get to them. You're not doing this."

Ah, the pretty sky eyes could flash angry sparks. Wyatt knew he shouldn't allow himself to be intrigued by her mercurial spirit, but what man wouldn't be? The woman was like an erratic fire, burning low and warm one minute, then leaping to an eager flame when something entranced or challenged her.

"Let me rephrase that in a less condescending way," he

said. "You're off the clock now, and that means you're not answerable to me, but if my presence won't be unwelcome, I'll show you Las Vegas up close."

Alex hesitated. Then she raised one brow. "Do you really expect me to tell my boss that his presence would be unwelcome?"

He fought the urge to smile…and then he lost the battle. "Actually, yes, I do. As I mentioned, you're on Alexandra time now. You call the shots."

She studied him. "You don't have to be my bodyguard."

Bad choice of words. It made him far too aware of how attracted he was to her curves and her pretty long legs. None of that changed the fact that sending Alex out with nothing but a map, a smile, innocent blue eyes and a can of hairspray buried in her purse would be an invitation to men with the wrong things on their minds. Men like him…except he was *not* going to touch her. *And that's an order, McKendrick.*

"If I'm asking you to point out the sights of my city, then it's only right that I should show you that city."

She opened her mouth, no doubt to give him another out.

"Alexandra," he said, "let's go."

"Is that an order from my boss?"

He frowned. "That's a request from an impatient…"

Man, he'd been going to say. "Tour guide," he finished a bit lamely. He could not begin to think of them as man and woman.

"Well, then," she said with a wide smile. "Lead on, tour guide. And make it good."

Wyatt wanted to groan. He glared down at her fiercely.

Immediately she looked contrite. "Too much? Out of line?"

He slowly shook his head. "It's your night."

She nodded. "I'll make it up to you tomorrow."

He couldn't help himself. He arched an eyebrow.

A pretty trace of rose suffused her cheekbones. "I meant that since I'll be more comfortable in my job tomorrow, it will pay off with the customers."

"You've been...uncomfortable?"

"Just a little—and only because I'm still getting my bearings and learning both the city and the hotel. I know you said that you'd handle any difficulties, but I need to handle things myself, you know?"

A loner like him? He understood the drive to be self-sufficient all too well.

"All right. We'll take care of that."

She smiled, and they left the building. He had his car brought around. "We'll walk part of the way later," he promised, handing her inside.

For several minutes they rode in silence.

"This awards situation," Alex suddenly said. "Now that I've been on the job a couple of days I'm curious. You played it down the other day, but obviously McKendrick's means a great deal to you. Do you really not care if you win or not?"

Her question caught him off guard. He thought back to all the times when he'd been told that he was less than nothing and that he would *never* be worth anything.

"I want to win," he admitted.

"A lot?"

He didn't want to think how much he needed to win. Thinking about it made him think of times he didn't want to remember.

"Wyatt?"

"A lot. Too much. It's just a meaningless award." But it was more than that to him.

"Okay. We'll win," she said.

"You say that as if it's that simple."

"Maybe it is, if we treat it as if it is. I'm a big believer in affirmations, at least where the obstacles aren't impossible to overcome." For a second, a tiny shadow seemed to turn those sky eyes darker. Or maybe he'd been mistaken. Her smile held.

He gave her an incredulous look. "Were you always this… optimistic?"

"You meant to say naive, didn't you?"

Wyatt studied her. "I meant to say that I appreciate your enthusiasm for the task." The sparkling smile she gave him warmed him more than was safe.

"All right, enough about awards. I'm going to give you a whirlwind tour. Las Vegas in a night," he said, trying to turn his thoughts from Alex.

He began with a quick tour of some of the major hotels that would have left experienced speed-daters short of breath. Walking her around the grounds of each hotel, he pointed out the things that would appeal to visitors. They visited the Eiffel Tower, the waterfalls at the Mirage. Alex gazed up at the black glass pyramid at the Luxor.

"I feel like a tourist," she said, taking a picture.

"You *are* a tourist." He tried not to smile, but lost the battle when she turned mock-indignant eyes on him.

"Not for long. With this great tour I can feel myself turning into Super Concierge already."

And when he took her to see the canals and gondolas and strolling performers at the Venetian, she touched his sleeve. "It's wonderful," she said.

Her eyes shone, and Wyatt found himself wanting to find ways to bring her smile out in full force, which would be…amazing…exciting…too much, he reminded himself. *Back off, McKendrick,* he ordered. Getting too close to Alex wouldn't be good for either of them.

"The vintage cars here belonged to celebrities and historic figures, heads of state," he said, pointing out the auto collection at the Imperial Palace, his voice droning on as if he wasn't totally aware of the woman at his side in a way that was perfectly…physical.

"It's a museum," she said.

He could tell by the way she automatically looked toward her little pink purse that she wanted her notepad, but then she shook her head and gave all her attention to the cars.

"Of sorts," he agreed. "But the cars are actually for sale to those who have enough money, and people do pull out their millions and buy them every day."

She laughed. "I'll start saving my millions tomorrow. Just as soon as I have my shop paid for."

Wyatt was glad she'd said that. It was good to be reminded how temporary she was.

"Last hotel," he said, leading the way. "One of the finest in the world."

"It's beautiful," she agreed, as they paused before the fountains of the Bellagio. "But you said it was one of the finest, and I know that's a title you covet for McKendrick's… So I guess I don't understand tonight's tour. You have a totally gorgeous and amazing hotel. Why show me the ones I won't be sending people to?"

He held out his hands, as if to concede her point. "But you might send them here for some things—a restaurant, a view, a good photo op. It may not make sense to promote a competitor's wares, but it's all about giving the customer the perfect experience. No one hotel does it all. If a customer is looking for something we don't have, I'll provide it by sending them elsewhere during their stay with us. In the end it pays off. They tend to remember that we were willing to bend over backward, including letting them escape our clutches for a few hours, to ensure their satisfaction, and they return to us. It works. Besides, placing too many restrictions on people tends to backfire."

His mouth was set in a hard line. This was obviously something he felt strongly about.

She wondered if that was why he was a loner. Because relationships placed too many restrictions on him? But of course Wyatt's personal life was none of her business, was it?

Wyatt followed up the hotel tour with trips to a few of the local sights. An amusement park, a quick drive past a museum.

"There are also helicopter tours. The city is something else, all lit up and seen from above. The colors against the dark sky are intense."

"I never knew Las Vegas had this much to offer," she said.

Her enthusiasm made him want to show her more…which was a definite sign that he should end the tour.

"One more thing this evening," he said, and then wished he hadn't said it. It made it sound as if there would be other nights, which wasn't wise. He was here tonight only because he'd been concerned for Alex's safety.

At least he hoped that was true. This had to be a one-night show. He didn't fraternize with many people, and certainly not with his employees. People could get hurt. Then there would be regrets attached to his home and his business.

"So…are we going to a mystery destination?" Alex asked, her voice breaking the silence at last.

"We're almost there. The sun is at just the right angle at this time of day."

She chuckled. "Is this like one of those movies where the sun shines through a break in the rocks, bounces off something, and magically opens the entrance to a secret cave? We certainly seem to be out in the middle of nowhere."

"Not exactly nowhere," Wyatt said, wishing Alex's little chuckle wasn't so low and sexy. "We'll only be an hour outside of the city. I promise this will be special, Alex."

Within minutes he heard her gasp as the sun hit the stark ancient red rocks that stretched out before them. The stone was gold and crimson and deep orange where the sun's rays caressed the rock, and shadowy black where the rays couldn't reach. "It's—that's *so* beautiful. What's it called?"

"It's the Valley of Fire, the oldest state park in Nevada and my favorite day-trip."

"It's wonderful. A good place to recommend to people who want to get away. Is that why you brought me here?"

Her question caught him off guard. He didn't have a clue why he had brought her here. Originally he'd told himself that he was trying to show her as many sights as he could, but now he suspected that he'd been hoping for that gasp at the first sight of his favorite retreat. Which had nothing to do with work.

That made it personal and unacceptable. She was his employee, in his care. What was more, she'd been so hurt by men that she'd given them up, and *he* certainly had nothing to offer her. Still, they were here, so he drove to some of the more scenic areas along the road.

"Look, people are getting married," she said, gesturing to a woman in a white wedding dress, her groom slipping a ring on her finger.

Alex's comment almost made Wyatt smile. "People are always getting married everywhere in Las Vegas, and in every way imaginable," he reminded her. "But, yes, this is a well-known wedding destination."

"Do you have many weddings at McKendrick's? I saw a

picture of the hotel on the Internet last night. Before it was yours it was a sad little place. No one would have gotten married there."

"They do now. It just needed some tweaking."

She laughed.

"What?"

"*Tweaking* is far too tame a word for what you've done with the hotel. It's unique and beautiful."

Okay, how could he not smile at that? "Are you sure you're not a bit biased?"

"I'm *totally* biased in some ways," she conceded, "but not in every way. I try never to let my personal feelings over-shadow my common sense."

It was, Wyatt thought, something that should have made him feel better. Instead it intrigued him. He wanted to know her better. That could be dangerous. Already he was doing things with her that he never did with any woman.

Like smiling, teasing, wanting to get closer than was wise.

And when they returned to the hotel, and he took her hand to help her out of the car, he had an aching desire to raise her hand, place his mouth on her palm, kiss her fingertips and pull her into his arms.

Instead he merely held her hand a second too long, and she looked as if he'd burned her.

That was a warning. He could hurt Alex. He didn't want to hurt her. He wanted to kiss her.

"Good night, Alexandra." He forced himself to walk away.

But somewhere in the night he woke remembering her smile, her scent, her soft skin…which was totally unaccept-able. Alex Lowell wasn't for him. She was an employee, an emotional woman, and he had ripped that kind of thing from his life years ago. He needed and wanted no one.

Still, the thought of Alex's soft voice seduced him. He stepped out onto the balcony of the penthouse, hoping for distraction in the night scene below. Clamping his hands on the railing, he stared into the darkness for a very long time.

Working with Alexandra Lowell was going to be a challenge.

CHAPTER SEVEN

ALEX'S mind was a torrent of activity. She tried not to remember Wyatt's rare smile last night, how it had felt to be alone with him as the sun's rays hit the red rocks, what his touch had been like.

Grr. He'd merely been helping her from the car. It had simply been two hands touching…and this was the second time she'd had this reaction. What was wrong with her?

Nothing. Ignore those absurd longings. That's guaranteed heartbreak. Don't throw common sense away. You know what's happened before when you've got involved with men you were trying to help, so back away from Wyatt. Don't think of him as a man. Concentrate only on what Wyatt wants for McKendrick's.

"Easy," she muttered. "Tweaking, positive change, winning a National Travel Award and total hotel domination."

A passing guest gave her a strange look. "What did you say?" the woman asked.

Alex blinked. She was losing it. She'd really said those words out loud, hadn't she? She could only hope that she hadn't also mumbled any of that stuff about Wyatt. If she had, Randy would be raising his bets, gambling that she *would* fall in love with Wyatt.

"I said that anyone who wants a tour should sign up on this sheet," Alex improvised, pulling some McKendrick's stationery from the desk. "Hotel Tour," she scribbled at the top.

"Oh, I didn't know they gave tours," the woman said. "I haven't seen half of what's here. Who's leading the tour? Are you?"

Uh-oh. Alex hadn't thought that far ahead. She just hadn't wanted the woman to think that Wyatt had hired a strange woman who talked to herself, so she'd simply blurted out that announcement. If she'd had time, she would have found someone better informed than she was to handle the task. As it was...

"Yes. I hope you'll consider coming along. This hotel has some amazing nooks and crannies," she said, even as she cringed at what she was saying. McKendrick's private spaces that weren't on the hotel map were a testament to the hotel's very private owner, but Alex hadn't yet located everything.

Time to pick Randy's brain. If she was promising a tour, then she was darn well going to do it right.

"I wouldn't miss it," the woman said, scribbling down her name. "You should put up a sign."

"That's an excellent idea," Alex said, and she set about making a temporary sign.

Within the next hour five more people signed up. Another couple was just putting their names down when Alex felt Wyatt's presence behind her. She didn't even question how she knew it was him. There was a change in the atmosphere, as if the air was supercharged. She turned around to find him examining her in that slightly distant, arch, bemused way he had.

Immediately her nerve-endings started to hum. It was a warning. Dangerous man ahead.

Wyatt looked at the sign, and when the couple moved away, he leaned in and put his name on the signup sheet.

"You don't need a tour," she said.

"No, but I'm interested in seeing what this one is like."

"I'm going to keep it simple. At least this first time. Later, I'll explore every inch of McKendrick's I've missed."

"Simple and safe can be good, but from what little I've seen, that doesn't appear to be your style. And you'd miss the private solarium." He grabbed a map and a pen and circled an unmarked place on the map. "It's a bit difficult to find, but worth the trip. And you wouldn't want to pass up the private dining rooms that are perfect for the man who wants a place to propose to the woman of his dreams." His voice had dropped low. "Would you?" he asked.

She slowly shook her head. "No, but I might need some help finding those."

"That won't be a problem."

"I don't understand."

He looked confused. "I *do* know my way around my own hotel."

"No. I meant that I don't understand why you went to so much bother about the romantic dining rooms. You don't believe in happily ever after."

"Not for me, no. But my customers find such touches appealing, and I try to give them what they want."

Alex hoped Wyatt never tried to give *her* what she wanted, because right now she wanted him to move closer.

As if he had read her mind, he did just that. "I'll meet you here at five," he said.

"I'll count on that."

He raised one eyebrow.

"I *really* might need some serious help. I don't even want to explain to you how this whole tour idea came about."

"Then I won't ask. But I *will* be there."

Alex felt like a moth trying to stay away from the seductive flame and knowing that she was losing the battle. She was going to be spending more time with Wyatt when only minutes ago she had determined to keep her distance.

And yet five o'clock suddenly seemed too far away. She was starting to show definite signs of "Wyatt fascination."

Randy would tell her that he'd told her so if she gave in. He might even actually win some money in the betting pool.

No, he won't, Alex thought. She might be fascinated by Wyatt, but that was as far as this woman was going to go. She'd walked into heartbreak before, but there had been justification then. This time there was absolutely none. It would be like taking a knife and intentionally stabbing herself. She just couldn't do it.

Just to make sure she remembered that, Alex grabbed a calendar from her drawer. Belinda had called to confirm that two months would be enough maternity leave. And with three days already gone, that left only fifty-seven.

Alex crossed a day off and wrote "57" on today's date.

There—she was back in charge of herself. But when the clock struck five, butterflies began an intense dance in her stomach. She turned to see Wyatt walking toward her.

I am totally betting against myself, she thought.

Wyatt was enjoying himself more than was wise. Alex had made a full confession about how the tour idea had been born. And now she was being completely charming with the guests.

"This is the Blue Ballroom," she said with a sweep of one arm. "It's named, I assume, for obvious reasons." She looked at Wyatt, a "hmm" expression in her eyes. "Maybe you could hire someone to choose a more imaginative name. Or have a contest to rename the room, with tickets to a local show as a prize."

"Oh, that would be fun! I have some great romantic ideas. Something to do with hearts or beating hearts or blues in the night," a woman said, followed by several other people agreeing.

And suddenly, McKendrick's was running a "Rename the Blue Ballroom" contest.

"I love your enthusiasm," Alex said, "and since this is a ballroom, well…if anyone feels like dancing, we'll stop here for a song or two. Pete, can you hit the music and the lights, please?" she called out to the custodian. Suddenly the crystalline chandeliers descended from the ceiling, their lights set to a perfect glow. Alex reached for Wyatt's hand as a low, sultry tune began to stream from the speakers. "I'm sorry, but we have to be the ones to start," she whispered.

He nodded. "Not a problem." Although, in fact, it was.

Touching Alex was like juggling flaming swords. Sooner or later a man was bound to set the curtains on fire and start something he couldn't stop. That wasn't allowed, but…what could he do? She had clearly gotten into this tour without thinking, and now she was improvising and treading water. Only someone with no heart at all would desert her now. He, it seemed, still had a heart…or something that vaguely resembled one. It had withered because he chose not to use it. With good reason, he reminded himself. Still, he would dance with her.

"How did this happen? The speakers and the music?" he asked, trying to keep his mind on the situation and off the woman.

She looked down at their joined hands as if she hadn't realized that she had taken his hand and was regretting the intimate connection. "I threw myself on Pete's mercy. I had to do something to give the tour a little oomph," she said. "Even if this whole event was…accidental, the guests signed up for a tour, and they deserve something special."

"I agree. So we'll dance, Alexandra." As he placed his hand at her waist, he was instantly aware of the warmth of her body, the subtle jasmine scent of her hair, those pretty blue eyes gazing up at him as he twirled her around the floor.

"I didn't actually plan this part beforehand. Us dancing together, I mean," she confessed. "I should have asked first, before roping you into this dance."

"Don't apologize. That's an order. Besides, I consider myself lucky. This may be my last chance to dance in the Blue Ballroom before it becomes the Beating Heart Ballroom," he said, surprising himself once again by teasing her. What was it about Alex that made him do such unwise things?

She chuckled. "I never thought about that. What if all the names submitted are hideous?"

"Then we'll have another contest."

"You're being very nice about being dragged into this," she said, but he shook his head.

"I believe I'm the one who dragged *you* into this job."

"I could have said no," she whispered as the music became slower. And without thinking, without a trace of common sense, he pulled her closer and tried not to think about how soft she felt against the hard planes of his chest.

She *could* have said no and left him in the lurch. But she had said yes, he thought, and now she was in his arms, and he was in danger of doing something stupid…like pulling her even closer against his body, right in front of the tour group.

But the music ended. Alex smiled and thanked him.

"There's nothing to thank me for. We danced. I enjoyed it." End of story. At least his mind wanted it to be the end. His nerve-endings, however, were still remembering Alex in his arms.

"Could we have another longer dance some evening?" someone asked.

"Why not weekly?" Alex suggested, and a new McKendrick's tradition was born.

The rest of the tour followed the same pattern, with Alex thinking of some new idea, such as having movies running constantly in the theater, complete with popcorn. But when they came to the solarium, she asked Wyatt to explain the history of the room.

"It was simple," he said to his audience. "When I first came here I missed green. So I tried to create a green haven."

"You succeeded," Alex said. "Tropical plants, comfortable chairs, private nooks and the sound of bubbling water. I could find a happy escape here."

"I hope you *will* come here when you need some downtime," Wyatt said, looking directly into Alex's eyes.

"Thank you," she mouthed silently, and he wasn't sure if she was thanking him for talking to the group or for suggesting a private escape for her. It didn't matter. What mattered was that for a moment he'd felt intimately connected to her. That wasn't safe for either of them.

By the time the tour ended, Alex was on a first-name basis with every person, and they had all promised to recommend the tour to others, to show up to her dances, to watch her movies and start submitting names for the ballroom. Within less than a week Alex had charmed his customers and promised to tip McKendrick's operating procedures upside down.

And, Wyatt mused as he insisted on walking her to her room, she had threatened the even keel he liked to maintain on his emotions. "You won them over easily," he told her as they made it to her door.

"Well, I have a lot of practice shepherding people around, and I enjoyed doing this. Helping people can be pretty rewarding most of the time."

"But not always?" There was that fleeting shadow in her eyes again.

"Nothing works one hundred percent of the time," she said. "Sometimes I get a little overzealous or overly involved and that can have a downside."

He wondered if she'd been "overly involved" with any of those jerks who had made her swear off men. But of course she had. Even from the short time he'd known her, Wyatt could see that Alex was the type to jump in and help total strangers. How much more would she give to those she cared about? And how deeply would she have been hurt when those men she'd cared for disappointed her?

That, he realized, was hitting too close to home. *He'd* disappointed women. He didn't want Alex to be one of them.

"That won't happen here, though," she told him. "I won't get…overzealous. I'm just trying to help the hotel."

She would have heard the stories about him and women. He knew about the bets. He ignored them.

"I'm glad you're here helping," he said, wanting to reassure her, to tell her that he wouldn't disappoint her.

"I'm glad, too. McKendrick's is so special."

At that husky comment about the place that he had poured himself into, Wyatt couldn't seem to stop the rush of sensation sluicing through him. "Thank you." He reached down, took her chin in his hand and lowered his head to taste her lips.

She was soft…warm…yielding. And when she angled her head and placed her hand on his chest, all reason fled. He pulled her to him, deepening the kiss. His senses were spinning.

She looped her arms around his neck. Her fingertips slid into his hair.

That small move nearly undid him completely, even as he realized that they were standing in the damned hallway!

As if he'd said something—*had* he whispered something against her lips?—Alex turned statue-still. She pushed back lightly against his chest with both palms. Immediately she stepped away.

"I'm sorry. I can't do this. I—"

Instantly, regret and anger at himself assaulted him. He reached out and took both her hands in his. "Shh, Alex. Don't apologize when I'm the one at fault. You've told me that you're on a break from men, so this was all on me. I should never have touched you."

"It *wasn't* just you," she insisted. "Although…yes, I do have a bad history with men. And I don't want to repeat that bad history. I'm absolutely *not* doing that anymore."

"You shouldn't."

"I won't."

"Good." He tipped her chin up with one finger. "If I ever step out of line, I want you to tell me. Don't let the fact that I'm your boss stop you. I've had enough vindictive people in my life to ever want to be one, so you're safe. All right? You'll tell me?"

He was expecting her to do something meek. She was clearly vulnerable right now. Instead she looked up, a mischievous expression lit her eyes, and she laughed. "You have got to be kidding. I can't think of too many women who would think you were getting out of line for merely kissing them."

He frowned. "I went from dancing with you straight to kissing you, and it was turning rather…fiery."

Her smile froze. "Yes, it was."

"I was on the verge of taking it further."

Alex looked to the side. "Um, well, yes, I was on the verge, too. And that's my point," she said, taking a visible

breath and looking at him again. She reached out and
tapped him on the chest with her index finger. Actually
poked him. "This isn't about what you were doing. This is
about me being in control of myself and knowing my limits.
I am and I do."

"Of course."

"I mean it. I'm *not* doing something stupid with you."

She sounded so incensed and miffed that he couldn't help
smiling. "Understood."

"Under no circumstances am I kissing you again or getting
all hot and bothered or…"

"Yes."

Alex looked directly into his eyes. She crossed her arms.
"Well, I think it's been a very full day, Mr. McKendrick, with
more to do tomorrow. I think I'd better go inside now."

"Of course," he said. "I agree. Good night, Alexandra." His
tone was totally calm. He sounded as if he had been completely unaffected by what had just happened here. He *wanted*
to be unaffected, had to be. But as he left her, heat still pulsed
through him. He wanted to kiss her again.

Alex was trying her best not to think about what had happened
last night, but every time she tried *not* to think about Wyatt,
her lips burned, her arms ached, her whole body…yearned.

"Stupid," she muttered.

"Something wrong?" Randy asked.

"Nothing," she lied. If her body had been a building, flames
would have been shooting through the roof.

"I just heard through the grapevine that the owners of
Champagne are upgrading all of their furnishings and offering
a complimentary chocolate dessert buffet for their guests
every night. They're determined to win the award."

"Does Wyatt know?"

"Wyatt knows everything, but if it matters to him he's not showing it."

But Alex knew that it mattered. McKendrick's was his creation, a wonderful creation. Why shouldn't he care?

"You stupid kid! You idiot!"

The yell came from across the lobby. A harried-looking mother with a baby and two little ones cried out as a man rose up above a small boy of maybe five. The little boy looked up in fear. An empty soda cup lay at his feet, a puddle of liquid pooling over a stack of papers. "This is my *work*. Lady, your stupid kid has ruined days of work, and I—"

The cords on the man's neck stood out. The boy cowered against his mother, who tried to reach out to him, but she was hampered by having her arms full with her other children.

"It's okay, Denny," she said, trying to substitute soothing words.

"It's not okay," the man said, bending over to get into the child's face. "You're an idiot, you know that? It's going to take me weeks to replace all of this."

Alex could hear the boy whispering loudly, "Sorry, sorry, sorry, sorry." Teary, desperate puffs of words. Her heart cracked. Anger rose up within her.

There was someone heading straight toward the concierge desk, obviously in need of assistance, but Alex didn't even stop to see who it was. She flew across the lobby toward the little boy, squeezing herself between the man and the child and jostling them both in the process.

"Don't listen, sweetheart," she told the boy in a soft, low voice. "I'm sure it was just an accident. They happen. To all of us."

"Butt out, lady," the man said. "It's not just an accident to me. I want somebody to fix this. Now. And I want his parents to pay me for what this little jerk did."

She felt the man's big, hard hand close around her bicep, but she didn't turn to look at him, even though her heart was beating fast. The little boy looked as if he was going to faint. His mother was starting to cry and desperately trying to find someplace safe to put her younger ones so she could get to her son.

Alex heard a woman gasp. Turning to look, she saw Wyatt moving toward her, his eyes like missiles targeted on the man.

"If you don't get your hand off her right now and back away from that child, you're going to find yourself in police custody very quickly. Almost immediately. I can guarantee that."

Wyatt's low but deadly voice cut through the crowd and a silence fell over the room. His expression was dark and fierce, his eyes narrowed. They flickered only slightly as he took in Alex and the boy and seemed to decide that they were all right. Then, as she quickly took the little boy by the hand and led the mother and her children over to a nearby couch, Wyatt turned his attention fully to the red-faced man.

"My papers are ruined," the man whined.

"That's regrettable. It's unfortunate that you don't have copies." But Wyatt's voice sounded anything but sympathetic.

"I do, but not here."

"Yet you terrorized a child, one of my guests."

"*I'm* one of your guests."

Wyatt's eyes were green ice. "Not anymore. Any money you've spent here will be refunded, but you're not welcome at McKendrick's."

"I have a reservation."

"And I have a hotel. My hotel trumps your reservation. Get out." He gave one quick look to the side, and instantly two security guards stepped out of a nearby foyer.

The man muttered a low, foul epithet, but he began to gather up his soggy papers as the guards approached. Wyatt asked another employee to take down the man's information. Then he turned to Alex, the woman and the little boy.

The woman looked as if life had been beating her up lately. "I— Thank you," she said to Alex and Wyatt. "Oh…here, I'll take her." The woman's littlest moppet— maybe three years old at best—had crawled onto Alex's lap, her thumb in her mouth.

"It's all right. She's fine," Alex said, stroking the child's silken curls. "She's adorable. And so is Denny."

Denny hung his head.

"He's clumsy now and then," his mother said, still a bit teary, "but he's a good boy."

"And he's very brave," Wyatt said, squatting down in front of the child. "Accidents happen, son," he said. "When I was your age, they happened to me all the time."

The boy's eyes widened. "For real?"

The desperation in his voice made Alex remember what it was like to be very young and do something humiliating in public. Children hadn't yet learned how to shrug that kind of thing off. The shame could resurface in thoughts years later.

"Oh, yeah," Wyatt said. "I once spilled red fruit punch on my uncle's white suit. It was his favorite, and I ruined it."

"What happened?" the boy whispered.

Wyatt hesitated. "I grew up. You will, too. You should be careful, but the man was wrong to talk to you like that. All of us make mistakes. He'll survive."

He lightly tapped the boy's nose, then turned to the mother, found out that she was visiting her sister at the hotel, and made arrangements for a meal and a babysitter.

After the woman and her children had gone upstairs, Alex

turned to Wyatt. She wanted to thank him for stepping into a situation that had been escalating. But Wyatt was already almost out of the vicinity. As he started to leave the lobby, he turned and looked at her, and there was a scowl on his face.

Maybe he didn't like having to get involved in the personal lives of his guests, maybe he was worried that this event would cost McKendrick's the award or…maybe he was worried that she was still remembering last night's kiss and would expect things of him now.

"Don't worry. That's not going to happen," she whispered, but of course he didn't hear her. He was already gone, and as usual he was alone.

The way he liked it, she reminded herself, remembering what Randy had told her.

CHAPTER EIGHT

A WEEK had passed, and Alex had grown into her job so quickly that she was starting to feel as if she really belonged at McKendrick's—something that was alarming, because she *didn't* belong. McKendrick's was too closely tied to Wyatt, a man who made her remember how it felt to be in his arms every time she saw him.

Just like a lot of other women had, she reminded herself. And a woman with her record certainly knew better than to travel that route. She wanted to help Wyatt's hotel win. Because it was a wonderful place, because Wyatt wanted to win and because…well, because she just wanted to. But her involvement had to stop at the hotel.

So she did her best to focus on McKendrick's, on the ballroom that was being renovated, on the reporters who had heard about the hotel's finalist status and had come to take pictures twice already. The thing *not* to concentrate on was the fact that Wyatt hadn't come near her since the day after their kiss. He'd clearly concluded her training and was on to other things. So she shouldn't be thinking of the man at all, except…

She could still see Wyatt with that little boy. The loner who had told her that he wasn't meant for marriage and children, who was clearly uncomfortable dealing with emotional people, had set aside his personal preferences to bond with and comfort a wounded child. If she thought about how she had felt watching Wyatt in that moment…Alex's heart tipped crazily. Visions of all the leaps she'd made into doomed love slammed into her soul.

Don't remember how you felt. Never let down your guard on your heart, she ordered herself. *Just work.*

She did. She drove herself. And when Wyatt sent around a memo that all employees were to take regular breaks and lunches, she took a five-minute break and a ten-minute lunch. A part of her knew that taking this job had been a huge mistake, but she had agreed to it. Now all she could think was that if she kept working the days would pass. Belinda would return, all this would end, and the worst that would have happened would be that Alex had melted in Wyatt's arms once. Surely she could survive that one mistake?

As long as she didn't stop to think, she'd be fine. Because thinking led to recalling the sound of Wyatt's voice. It led to reliving the sensation of Wyatt's mouth on hers.

The kiss had been a mistake, as he had said, but it had felt too wonderful—and had made her want more.

"Grr," she told herself.

At Randy's questioning look, she automatically held up a piece of paper. "You wouldn't believe some of the suggestions for the new name of the ballroom."

"I could help you with that."

She blinked. "Thank you. You're a good guy, Randy."

He blushed. Actually blushed. "Just doing my job."

"Well, you do a great job. I may need help if we get too many more of these. For now I'll let them sit. I have to map out a tour for the Airinson group. They'll be here at two." She glanced at the list she was making.

At that moment Randy's phone rang. He picked it up. "Yes. No. She took a lunch break. How long? Well…"

He mumbled a few more things Alex didn't catch, and when he hung up he gave Alex one brief, evasive look, then turned away.

Five minutes later Wyatt strode across the lobby with Jenna, who worked in the office, skip-stepping to keep up.

"Come on," Wyatt said to Alex. "Time to get your basic nourishment. I don't want you keeling over at your desk."

"I had lunch."

"I heard about your ten-minute lunch. And that you were interrupted by a phone call. Let's go."

He looked down at the overflowing contest basket and at the stacks of paper on her desk. The collection of cute little personal items and photos she kept there was almost obscured.

"Enforced downtime just arrived," he told her. "Tell Jenna what's a priority. Randy will back her up if she needs help."

Since Randy was obviously the one who had ratted her out, Alex looked up at him. "*You* have a big mouth," she told him.

"Don't blame Randy. You can't skip meals or work non-stop," Wyatt told her, "and Randy had his orders."

To her amazement Randy was looking guilty. "I know you were just trying to help," she told him.

"You do a great job, but you work too hard."

It was the nicest thing he had said to her. "You're a sweetie, Randy," she said.

He looked horrified. "Don't tell."

"It's just between the four of us," she promised. "Let me finish this tour map," she told Wyatt. "The Airinsons are counting on me. Then I'll eat."

Wyatt gave her an exasperated look. "The Airinsons will find free tickets to a show in their room and an apology from me for pulling you off the job. Jenna will make a great map for them."

"I promise I'll do my best, Alex," Jenna said.

"Okay. I'll get the rest of my lunch." Alex reached for a drawer.

"No need. I'm taking you out of here." Wyatt's jaw was rock-solid, his look grim. Something was wrong.

Alex stopped arguing and followed him.

He handed her into his black sports car and drove to an exclusive, out of the way restaurant. She looked at the prices on the menu and flinched.

"Thank you for taking me to lunch, but I— Why are you looking like a thundercloud?"

"This isn't working."

Her heart fell. "I told you the first day that I might not be the right person for the job."

He glared at her. "You *are* the right person."

"But you just said…"

"I didn't think I would have to drag you from the clutches of an insane jerk. Nor did I think I would have to kidnap you to get you to take a break. Most people stop working at designated times to rev their engines and just get some fresh air. That's why it's called a break, Alexandra."

Okay, now she saw the trouble. Wyatt took the hotel seriously. Everything about the hotel, including his employees' welfare. "I don't want you to worry about what happened the other day with that…that…"

"Gorilla," Wyatt supplied.

"He wasn't that big."

"He was a lot bigger than you." Oh, clearly this topic had been festering inside him.

"You could have simply come to me and forbade me from interfering in altercations between guests."

He gave her a "you've got to be kidding" look. "You're the woman who told me that you tend to be overzealous about helping people. You ignored my memos about breaks and lunches. You implied that you make decisions based on emotions."

"I did not."

"Didn't you? Well, somehow I must have just gotten that impression. Oh, yes, now I remember how. Maybe because you squeezed yourself in between that boy and the man, so that *you* would take the pummeling if he decided to let his fists fly."

"You would have done the same."

"Maybe." How ridiculous. Of course he would. The only thing that had saved that jerk of a man from a punch in the jaw had been the fact that Wyatt knew how to exercise self-control. Except when he was tasting a woman's lips.

Alex frowned to herself, but Wyatt had moved on.

"It doesn't matter if I would have, anyway. I'm taller, bigger and stronger than you. He could have hurt you."

"But I'm fine."

"You're not. You're pushing yourself and not getting away from your desk enough."

Again Randy's words about guilt nudged at her. "I don't want you to feel guilty just because I forgot to take much of a lunch break today. I was getting to it."

He gave a harsh bark of a laugh. "You," he said, pointing a breadstick at her, "are a workaholic."

She laughed and picked up her own breadstick. "You ought to know. You're one, too."

But he was still frowning. "Seriously, Alex. Cesar, who works the night desk, told me that you came downstairs the other day to help Lois out when things got busy, and then you slipped in two extra tour groups. After hours."

"Work is how—" she began, and then stopped. How could she put this? *Work is how I keep my mind off you?* Or worse...

Reality struck. Work, helping people, was how she'd always tried to impress those she cared about, the way she'd tried to win their affection. The possibility that she was doing that now made her ill; it totally frightened her. Because Wyatt was the one man she'd never even stood a chance of winning. He'd told her so. Randy had told her that. Everyone had told her. And yet she couldn't stop. With the awards, there was too much at stake. Reports of Champagne's new improvements were coming in daily.

"What does this award mean to you?" she asked.

He frowned. "It doesn't mean life or death," he said. "It doesn't mean I want you making yourself sick."

"Okay. I promise I won't make myself sick. I'll be reasonable."

He looked incredulous.

"I'll be *more* reasonable than I have been," she said. "Why do you want to win? Why are you working so hard to obtain it?"

His jaw tensed.

"Please," she said. "Tell me."

His eyes turned fierce and angry. "I don't want to want it, but I do. It would be...validation."

Something in his eyes reminded her of Randy's comment about Wyatt's past. *Let that be a warning*, she told herself. It had been a girl from Leo's past and a woman from her stepfather's past that had taken them out of her life. Men with dark, secret pasts had never been good for her. "I want to help you win," she said.

"And I want to win. But not by harming your health. I can't be abusive, Alex, demanding that everyone jump in an effort to make me happy. I don't want and I can't have a slave."

That cool edge that always tinged his voice was gone, replaced by something much more raw. Alex wanted to know what that was about, but Wyatt clearly didn't want to share anything that personal. And maybe… Was she afraid to know more? Afraid of what she might feel?

She studied him, looked down at the table, then up again.

"You don't have to worry. I won't be a slave for any man. I've willingly volunteered to be a lesser person before and I'm through with that. It hasn't worked out well for me. But nothing you've asked me to do falls into that category."

His green gaze held her captive. "You're going to have to explain that 'lesser person' part."

Alex tried to look away, tried to think of some light way to laugh and brush away this question. Opening her soul to Wyatt would be a mistake. It would be a connection…and there could be no connections with this man.

"Oh, you know, it was just one of those minor 'left over from my childhood' things. After you have not one father but two fathers walk out the door, you tend to try a little too hard to salvage your relationships. You give a little too much of yourself. I might have subverted my needs to others once or twice, but, as I said, that's completely in the past. It's irrelevant."

She had tried to say it in an offhand, breezy manner, but Wyatt wasn't looking breezy. "Elaborate on subverting your needs to others."

Alex considered sidestepping that command. She could have reminded him that he was being highhanded and that baring her soul wasn't a part of her job, but then she made the mistake of looking into those fierce green eyes. Her breath caught in her throat. Dizziness threatened. She wanted to lean closer, and suddenly talking seemed like the safest thing to do. Telling him about the stupid mistakes she'd made suddenly became a way to put some distance between them, to keep her mind off the man.

So, despite the fact that she didn't want to go into the humiliating details, she told him about tutoring Robert, mentoring Leo, and helping Michael with his parenting problems. "They thought they cared, but they were just…grateful and euphoric, I suppose," she said. "And once their self-confidence was restored, I was only a rung on the ladder, one that had served its purpose. They felt guilty, but it didn't change things. I learned a valuable lesson. So you really don't have to worry about me overdoing it at McKendrick's. I like the work, but I'm not volunteering for a servile position."

"Idiots," he said.

"I was making the point that you don't have to worry about me being a sacrificial lamb. I wasn't aiming for your pity. I was trying to tell you that helping you isn't hurting me. You're not taking advantage of me, because I know all about that and this isn't it."

"They wounded your spirit," he said angrily.

"But I survived."

"That's because you're an intelligent, competent, self-assured woman."

"Yes, I am," she said, and realized that it was true. Her bad luck with love hadn't broken her. Yet. "I'm not being egotistical. I know my flaws. But I also know what I like and what I'm good at, and that's connecting with people on a basic, friendly, let-me-help-you level. It's what drives me at work and what will help me get to where I want to be. I can help you win."

"By running yourself into the ground?"

She sighed. "Wyatt, weren't you listening? I thrive on work. It makes me feel good about myself. This job makes me feel powerful. To you I'm running myself into the ground. To me I'm just…being me."

Without thinking, she reached across the table and placed her hand on his. Bad mistake, since she was now totally physically aware of him. Her first thought was to jerk back, but then he'd know how much he was affecting her, so she didn't.

"I know my tendency to overdo makes people crazy. I did warn you about it that first day. But I'm not in any danger. I'm used to taking care of myself," she said. "I know how. When both my fathers left us, we were out on the street lots of times with no home. My mom was a mess, and I had to be the grown-up at times. So it's good of you to worry about me, but…"

He swore. Actually swore—even if it was beneath his breath. "You are driving me crazy," he told her. "*I* am not a good person. I have never been a good person. When I was growing up, my family members could barely control me. True, they were all first-class brutish animals, who detested the fact that I had even dared to survive my infancy, but they weren't completely wrong about me, either. I lived to make them miserable."

"Ah," she said. Now she saw…*something*—a small piece of Wyatt's past—and it filled her with pain. It involved a small boy and a much larger person bearing down on him. She remembered a comment Wyatt had once made about perfection. She remembered the moment with that guy the other day calling that little boy an idiot and Wyatt explaining how he had once made a lot of mistakes, too. "Your family wanted to change and control you." Somehow she kept her voice from breaking.

He glowered. "As you said, I didn't share this with you to earn your sympathy. I don't talk about this stuff…to anyone but you need to know that I'm not ever going to be the knight in shining armor type. I'm the fists flying, spit in your eye type, and without even thinking about it I could hurt you, Alex. I wouldn't want to, but it would happen anyway, so don't start getting that 'I'll take care of you' look in your eyes. I've seen you use that with customers."

"And you've liked it then."

"Yes, but I'm not a customer."

"You're my boss."

"Yes," he said. "I am. Most definitely." Her hand was still resting on Wyatt's. Now he flipped his palm over and took her hand in his own. "Don't make me worry about you."

Again she remembered what Randy had said about Wyatt becoming withdrawn when he broke a woman's heart. Was this where she repeated her past again? A man regretting he'd gotten too close, who now had to find the nearest exit? She was sure that Wyatt's withdrawal when he walked away from a woman was the result of the guilt he felt. A man who had been made to suffer, who had been denied love as a boy, would...would *what*?

Maybe he'd become an over-achiever, intent on proving that he deserved his place on the earth. Maybe he'd even want to accumulate accolades and awards to throw in their faces. And maybe...would he insulate himself by refusing to care about anyone deeply again? Good chance of that, and any woman who didn't understand was bound to get her heart shredded. Would he worry about being the cause of other people's pain? Oh, yes, it seemed he would. Because he would know too well what pain felt like.

"Have you really hurt women?" she asked, surprising herself and apparently surprising him, too, by his expression. He had just told her that he didn't share this stuff and shouldn't have shared what he already had. "I'm sorry. It was just a passing comment I heard. I shouldn't have mentioned it."

Wyatt sighed and frowned. "You should have if it was bothering you. And the answer is yes. And no. Not physically. Never. But emotionally? That's a big yes."

And it was clear that he hated that.

"All right. I'll try not to make you worry," she promised. "I'll set the alarm on my watch and I'll take my breaks. Randy will remind me. I won't get sick on your watch. I promise you that." *And I won't fall in love with you and bring that anguish to your eyes, either*, she silently promised. At least she wouldn't if she could help it. It was hard to resist a man who watched over his employees this carefully.

The darkness lifted from his expression, just a bit.

"But I have a good work ethic," Alex told him. "I've told you how much my work and my success and doing a good job means to me, how it empowers me. So…since I don't like taking too long for my lunch break we should eat." Because now she was totally conscious that he was still holding her hand. His thumb was caressing her palm. It felt…exquisite.

She stared at where he was touching her.

He let her go and shrugged. "My mistake."

Alex started to remind him that she was the one who had touched him first, but when she opened her mouth to say it, he stared at her with those fierce green eyes and she knew that he already knew what she was going to say.

He lifted one lazy eyebrow. "*My* mistake," he said again.

She nodded. "You're the boss," she told him again.

"Sometimes I wonder," he muttered, as the waiter came up and took their order.

But what Alex was wondering when she returned to work after lunch, was how she was going to maintain a professional distance from Wyatt now that she'd seen a glimpse of his soul. The urge to fix, to help, was kicking in. She knew that feeling, and she'd lived to regret it. The fact that her reaction to Wyatt was more intense than anything she'd felt before only made things worse.

Start planning your return to San Diego, she told herself. Good advice. She would take it. She picked up the phone and began to dial.

CHAPTER NINE

WYATT was in a foul mood. Remembering Alex's story and her attempt to be nonchalant about what had been done to her fueled an anger he didn't want to analyze. That anyone would hurt someone as sunny as Alex—she deserved better than that.

A good thing to remember, he reminded himself. Because he'd been thinking about her too much lately, and he wasn't one whit better than any of those men had been. He would hurt her just as easily as they had.

Something hot and painful sluiced through him. He shoved it aside. Alex was a prize for McKendrick's. *But she wasn't for him*, he reminded himself. He'd do well to remember that.

It was time to get back to thinking about the hotel and to stop thinking about Alex. Maybe he should simply pay her in full and hire someone less competent to stand in until Belinda could return.

But he knew that he wouldn't do that. He was as bad as any of the men who had harmed her. He *liked* what she did for McKendrick's. Worse than that, he liked sparring with her…and looking at her…and touching her. And, for the short time she was here, he was going to continue to enjoy all those things.

* * *

"Are you sure you're all right? You're looking a little flushed every time we mention Wyatt," Jayne said later that night. Alex was on a video call with Jayne and Molly. Serena wasn't around tonight—even though she'd returned to Las Vegas… to be with the man she'd married during their weekend. She and Alex had managed to catch up briefly a few days earlier, when she had called on Alex to help shop for an outfit suitable for a mayoral candidate's wife. How had *that* happened?

"I'm fine. Really. It's Serena I'm worried about. She really didn't seem like herself."

"I know. I get the impression she's confused. Not happy. I wish we had all stayed together that night," Jayne said.

Molly frowned. "Yes. Staying together would have been best."

Was there something in Molly's eyes other than concern for Serena? Alex couldn't tell. Darn video phone.

"I'm going to talk to her again as soon as I can," Alex said.

"Yes, but who's going to talk to *you*?" Molly asked.

"Molly, I promise if I get in too deep I'll tell you. So far I'm handling it."

A long silence ensued. "What's 'it', exactly?" Jayne asked.

Uh-oh. "I kissed Wyatt one day." Okay, he had kissed her. Same difference, since she had kissed him back.

"Alex…" Molly drawled.

"I'm good. I'm not letting it affect me. I'm totally over it," Alex said. Which probably wasn't the best thing to say. It implied that she had, in recent memory, *not* been over it.

"I don't like what I'm hearing…or not hearing, Alex." Molly's voice quivered. "Men can be such trouble."

"Men can wreck your life if you let them," Jayne said.

"But I'm strong. I know Wyatt isn't available, and I won't let anyone wreck my life." *Including me,* Alex thought.

"But Wyatt kissed you..." Molly prompted.

"Yes, but only in a lustful way, not a romantic way. It was—" the most intimate, expert kiss she'd ever had "—it was nice, but I'm safe. I'm not getting involved."

"You're repeating yourself, Alex. And somehow I don't feel better after this conversation," Jayne said.

"I do. I miss you guys. For your sakes as much as mine, I'll do a lot of counting to ten," Alex promised.

Her friends smiled. "If you need us, we've got your back."

"Thanks, you two. I'll get in touch with Serena."

Alex hung up the phone. Talking to her friends was a bit like talking to a mom these days. She loved them, she missed them, and she didn't dare tell them everything. If she did...

"They would worry themselves sick," she muttered. Just the way she was worrying about them.

Alex was particularly worried about Serena, so when her friend called and suggested that they meet at Hennesey's, an Irish pub, Alex jumped.

"I can't believe you're back here in Las Vegas," Alex said. "It's wonderful."

"It's so good seeing you," Serena agreed, which wasn't exactly the same thing. How *was* she feeling about being married? "Come on, let's move outdoors. The music's great, but I want to be able to hear what's happened to you."

"What's happened to *me*?" Alex launched into a description of some of the projects she'd started at the hotel.

"Jayne and Molly said that you and your boss kissed. Alex..."

"Serena..." Alex said, duplicating her friend's tone. "Or should I call you *Mrs.* Benjamin?"

Serena blinked. Then she laughed. "Okay, we're even—and aren't we a pair? How did life ever get this complicated?"

"I guess we came to Las Vegas and started a few things we hadn't anticipated starting." Alex took a sip of her drink as the lilting strains of music floated out on the breeze. "Do you love him, Serena? Does he love you?"

Serena hesitated. "It's… I'm not sure how this is all going to play out. How about you? How do you feel about Wyatt kissing you? I'm always interested to hear more about the virile one."

Alex laughed. "Let's just say that Wyatt could make a living giving kissing lessons if this hotel gig doesn't pan out. Still, it shouldn't have happened, and we've gotten beyond it."

Later, after Serena had opened up and talked about her husband, Jonas, just enough so that Alex was *really* worried about her friend's chances of ever having a happily-ever-after, Alex drove back to McKendrick's.

Had she really said that she'd gotten beyond the kiss with Wyatt? *When did I become such a liar?* she thought. And why was she lying to her friends?

Wyatt needed to get away. For the past two weeks he'd been measuring his every action, his motivations, his words. He should never have kissed Alex, because each time he got near her now, his entire body reacted. He envisioned her in his arms and in his bed, and it was time to put a stop to that. He needed to remember what he was all about…and what he was *not* about. He had to go somewhere away from the hotel and the world as he knew it. A place where there was no chance of glancing over to see what was going on with Alex. Because she wouldn't be there.

He was dressed casually, unusual for him, and as he walked toward the entrance, several women smiled and said hello. As always he was polite, but no more. He dated only casually, and he kept the hotel and his personal life separate. Maybe because the hotel meant more to him than anyone he'd ever dated had. His success in business didn't carry over to the rest of his life. After walking away from numerous women, he had realized that he didn't have the basic emotional tools to fall in love and maintain a relationship. That part of him had died long ago. Or maybe it had never existed.

Growing up, solitude, hiding, had saved him from beatings and abuse. He'd always been alone, because when he was young it had been the only way. And now?

It was *still* the only way. He'd never been able to make the leap to love, could never let anyone inside his walls, and he always ended up hurting some innocent woman. That made him loathe himself for being such a cold beast, so solitude was the life for him. Forever.

Normally he was fine with that, and today, as usual, he was on his own. He drove to the one place in Las Vegas where he didn't have to maintain his image. The Haven was an old motel with cottages and a small chapel, a rundown bit of property he'd bought a few years ago with the idea of fixing it up. But for some reason he never had. It was a place that drew him. Usually he could relax and lose himself in solitude there…except today he couldn't.

Lounging in a chair inside the one cottage where he'd made minimal improvements, he tried to read. And put down his book. Once. Twice. Three times.

"It's her," he said aloud, glancing at the red rocks in the distance, but seeing pretty blue eyes. Wyatt groaned. "I have to stop thinking of her," he muttered.

Because nothing had changed. He didn't want a relationship, and she'd been hurt in her relationships. She wanted a home. He didn't even live in a home. He had no knowledge of a real home. But what was she doing right now?

Most likely she was at her desk, very efficiently managing his guests. Issues with some of those visitors might be arising. And, even though it wasn't her job to handle customer disputes, some of his employees had been going to Alex lately if he wasn't available. Her ability to make people feel good, the way she smoothed things over easily, had people bending the rules. When he was at hand no one did that, but when he wasn't...

Wyatt slammed the book closed. Maybe he should have brought Alex with him. He wondered what she would think of the Haven.

She'd probably think it was a decrepit pile of rock and wood that needed to be torn down. She'd think less of him then. And that would effectively kill his fascination with her.

Next time, he promised himself. Next time he'd bring Alex. But for now...

"Rest time's over, McKendrick."

She should be feeling better about how her day was going, Alex conceded. She'd come up with two new activities to make McKendrick's stand out from the crowd. And, despite the fact that there'd been an article in the local paper yesterday about Champagne sponsoring some sort of exclusive event this weekend, the crowds at McKendrick's were just as big as ever. People looked relaxed and happy. She'd had nothing but good vibes from those approaching her desk this morning.

She'd hardly even noticed that Wyatt had left two hours ago, taking some rare time off, she told herself. Despite the fact that the hotel seemed emptier without him around, she was okay with that...wasn't she? It was normal to feel a little different when there was a change in one's routine.

Of course she *had* noticed that a few women gave him hopeful waves as he left. She'd even wondered if there might be another woman sharing his day off, and felt a stabbing pain near her heart, but she'd forced herself to try to ignore it.

She was almost succeeding, too, when she looked up to see a young maid headed toward Randy, then veering off when she saw that he had people at his desk. Alex had none, and the look of relief on the maid's face was palpable.

"I just passed the ballroom, and two of the workers doing the renovation are fighting," the young woman said.

"Physically?"

"No, but there's a lot of yelling. The customers can hear them. And the security guys are on the tenth floor, helping a woman who fell getting out of the bathtub. I didn't know what to do, so I came here."

"Thank you. It was the right thing to do," Alex said, and she took off toward the ballroom. She could hear raised voices before she even opened the doors.

"Don't worry," she told the crowd of people that had started to gather. "It's probably just a minor disagreement between friends. I'll straighten everything out."

She pulled open the tall double doors and walked into the huge, mostly empty room. At the far end, workers were involved in various tasks, but just twenty feet inside the room, two big muscle-bound men were right up in each other's faces, yelling and swearing and getting louder and more red-faced every second. They didn't even look away from each other when she entered the room.

Alex took a deep breath. She had no idea what to say or do. Her heart started tripping as she drew closer. No doubt she should call someone else, but who? The longer and louder these two got, the more agitated the customers outside the doors would become. If this accelerated into an actual fist fight, wouldn't *that* look great in the morning papers? She could practically see the headline: *Blood spilt at McKendrick's.* The owner of Champagne would waltz away with Wyatt's award.

She frowned. She was so *not* going to let that happen. She wanted Wyatt to win. At the moment she didn't even care why it mattered to her. She'd worry about that later. But for now…

Alex took a deep breath. She waded into the fray. "I don't know who you two are," she said, raising her voice just enough so that it carried, "but I'm here on Mr. McKendrick's behalf, and if you don't stop this right this minute, your firm will lose its contract. I'm giving you fair warning. I'm walking right up next to you, so if anyone hits anyone, I'll probably get hit, too. That will be assault, and you won't even be able to plead that you didn't know that I was here."

She kept moving as she spoke. "Who are you, anyway?" she asked. "And, no, I don't want to know what you're fighting about. I just want it stopped. Right now."

By now she was only three feet away, easily within the peripheral vision of the men. One of them blinked. He turned toward her. "This doesn't concern you."

"Yes, it does. My job is to make sure my customers are happy. You're scaring them."

The other man turned toward her. He looked her over, head to toe. "So you work for Mr. McKendrick. Who exactly *are* you, luscious lady?"

Alex realized that if the man wanted to, he was close enough to reach out and touch her. She took a very slight step back.

"I'm Alexandra Lowell."

"And she's none of your business." The deep, steely voice

came from behind Alex. She turned to see Wyatt, eyes blazing, bearing down on them. "I suggest you two men return to your work immediately," he said. "I'll discuss this with you and your supervisor shortly."

The man who'd asked who she was scowled and grumbled something unintelligible, but both of them turned. They started to lumber back to whatever they had been doing before all this began.

Wyatt waited until they were out of hearing range. "Break time?" he said, and Alex looked up into his glittering eyes. He was angry and not trying to conceal it.

"I'd say that's a yes. But I should…"

"Find someone to man your desk? It's already done. Let's talk," he said, his tone perfectly calm.

But Alex didn't miss the tense line of his jaw. She turned and followed him out of the ballroom and down the hallway. He threw open the door to a conference room, pulled her inside and then shut the door behind them.

"What was that?" Wyatt asked, trying to leash his anger.

"That was me trying to avert a crisis."

"That was you trying to get your pretty face and body re-arranged. Again. Presenting yourself as a punching bag to en-raged men is getting to be a habit, Alex. Do you *know* what one swing from one of those men's fists could do to you?"

"This is nothing like that other time. Protecting that little boy was…well, anyone would have done that."

Wyatt seriously doubted that. "So how is this different?" He gazed down into those sky eyes, waiting for her answer and for his heart to stop racing, but it didn't. Watching her confront two full-grown angry men, listening to one of them try to hit on her…he wanted to swear.

"Two reasons. For one, the hotel's reputation was at risk this time."

He lost the battle not to swear. "Alex, you're an amazing woman. You're doing great things for McKendrick's and you've become a customer favorite." *My favorite*, he thought, but he couldn't utter those words. He shouldn't even be thinking them. "But I don't want you to get hurt helping me." *I don't want to hurt you. I don't want to be another man taking your help and then not giving anything back.*

"Wyatt, I'm fine," she said. "Look." She held out her arms, as if to show him that she was all in one piece.

He raised an eyebrow. "Don't try to schmooze me, Lowell. You know what I mean. You're not to confront any more angry men. For any reason. Got that?"

For a second he thought she was going to do the right thing and meekly agree, the way any other employee would have. But Alex raised her chin and looked him square in the eye. "I'm sorry. I can't agree to that. If I'm going to run my own shop, one I operate alone, I have to be able to handle any situation. That was the second reason I had to get involved."

Wyatt growled. There was nothing he could say to that, was there? Except this. "I know you're going to run a fantastic shop. People will visit in droves. Every customer will go away satisfied. But don't practice your negotiating skills here, Alex. Not again. If any bullies come in and Security is otherwise occupied, you send them to me. If any workers get into an argument, you send them my way. Anything that might threaten you physically, you step away from. If I'm not here, you find someone bigger than you to handle it, and then you find me."

"It was your day off." She hadn't lowered her chin even a notch.

"Where your safety is concerned, I have no days off. Understood?"

She blinked.

"Alex? Please."

As if that one word did it, she nodded. "All right. Actually, I *was* just the tiniest bit concerned. When that one guy asked me who I was and looked at me as if he wanted to…do something, it made my skin crawl."

And any thought Wyatt had of regaining his composure flew right out the window. He slid his hand around Alex's waist and slowly drew her close, giving her ample time to tell him to stop or to push back. "I'm *not* going to let anyone touch you."

But Wyatt was most definitely touching her. He pulled her even closer. For a moment, several moments, he just held her. He stroked her hair and whispered soothing words against her temple. She was warm and vibrant and so…*Alex* in his arms that he couldn't stop himself from reacting to her, wanting her.

He drew back and gazed down into her eyes, his lips close to hers. "I'm going to kiss you, Alex."

"Yes." The word came out on a breath.

"You can stop me. You can say no. You know you have a choice."

Her answer was to rise on her toes and press her lips to his. "I know," she whispered against his mouth.

Heat seared him, desire flooded his soul, and he drew her closer. He kissed her again, opening his mouth over hers.

She met him, kissed him back.

He ran his hand down her spine, learning her curves.

She plunged her fingertips into his hair, licking his lips when they came up for air.

"Alex…" he groaned as he kissed her more, reached for more.

The door flew open. Without taking a breath, Wyatt immediately turned so that Alex was behind him and he was mostly blocking her from view. Jenna, who worked in the office, was standing there, along with several guests. His reaction, though quick, had obviously not been quick enough. They had seen Alex already, splayed up against his chest, locked in his arms.

As if on cue, Alex peeked out from beneath his arm. "Well, that was *so* great! Thank you so much for that demonstration of what I should do if anyone should try to sexually harass me, Mr. McKendrick. And that nifty move where I turn your thumb back and bring you to your knees? It's one I've heard about but I've never actually met anyone who would allow me to try it on them. I mean, I'm really sorry your hair got messed up when you ended up falling during the demonstration, but I assure you that all this stuff is going to be incredibly useful. A girl really needs to know a few tricks to protect herself from the bad guys. Hotels are not immune from these things, you know, Jenna," she said, shaking a warning finger at the woman. "Every guest should know at least a few basic moves."

Then, as if she was completely unaware of this surreal situation that everyone was trapped in, Alex got that amazing, intense lightbulb look in her eyes that Wyatt was beginning to recognize. "I think maybe we could offer some basic self-defense classes in the ballroom. Just in case anyone is interested. Wouldn't that be great? I'm going to get right on that."

Then she smiled at the tour group again and left the room, her usual spring in her step.

"A self-defense class? That's a wonderful idea, Mr. McKendrick—don't you think?" Jenna asked.

Wyatt blinked. He was angry at himself for putting Alex at risk, and it must have shown on his face.

"I'm sorry. Did I do something wrong?"

Wyatt wanted to groan. "No, Jenna. And, yes, it's a great idea. Alex has come up with another way to improve McKendrick's." What was he going to do when she had gone? he wondered, knowing he wasn't thinking only of the hotel. He frowned again, then remembered Jenna. "So…you think it will work?" he asked her, trying to be encouraging. Jenna hadn't been here very long. He didn't want her to think he was crazy. The CEO of Champagne would certainly *love* that, wouldn't he?

"Oh, I think it'd be great," Jenna said. "I'd totally sign up if they were held here. What could be more convenient?"

The people in the group agreed, although some of them still looked as if they weren't quite sure what had just happened.

Wyatt wasn't sure, either, but it was probably a good thing that Jenna had interrupted. He was completely losing his self-control where Alex was concerned.

He could still taste her. He wanted to go looking for her to finish what they'd started. Only two things stopped him. Alex had been hurt so badly in the past that she had walked away from men and love forever. And he was still the same man he'd been this morning. A loner. Incapable of maintaining a long-term relationship. If he couldn't offer her more than the disappointing men she'd already suffered through, then he didn't have the right to pursue her. He refused to be the next disappointing jerk in her life. He couldn't be the man who finally broke her spirit.

He wanted to *shore up* Alex's spirit. She'd had to handle a nasty situation. *His* contribution couldn't have made her day less trying, either. And if he was part of the problem…well, who did she have to share her troubles with? No one, it seemed. She was cut off from the home she loved, without her lifeline. There was no one with whom to discuss the problems her life as his concierge had brought about.

Wyatt swore. In the past couple of weeks he'd begun to learn
how Alex operated. She went all out to help people, and sometimes people—unscrupulous men—took advantage of her good
nature. *He* had taken advantage today, and once she had time
to think, she might beat herself up for letting him kiss her again.

In fact, too much had happened to Alex since he'd yanked
her out of the life she loved. She'd been pushed too far, thrown
into situations she never should have been forced to handle.
Alex needed backup, maybe even comfort.

For half a second he thought again about spiriting her away
to the Haven, his hideaway…a place he never showed anyone. But he immediately dismissed the idea.

That wasn't the right place for her, and he wasn't the right
person for the job. At all. But he knew who might be. Just because *he* had no need for friends didn't mean that he had
missed the fact that Alex *did* need them.

CHAPTER TEN

ANTICIPATION built within Alex as the limo dropped her off in front of Tableau, a restaurant located in an atrium, surrounded by pools. She opened the door and went inside.

Immediately she heard a squeal. "Alex!"

Molly came running up to her and gave her a big hug. Jayne and Serena were only steps behind.

Alex's throat clogged with happy tears. Somehow Wyatt had managed to fly Jayne and Molly out, and he'd located Serena and arranged this meeting.

She couldn't help wondering why. Wyatt's explanation had simply been that he knew she missed her friends. That seemed too simple, but she *did* miss them. And she needed to see them, to get her head on straight.

After Wyatt had kissed her crazy in the conference room the other day, she'd gone to her room, bent over to keep from fainting and prayed she would get a brain, get a clue, and stop longing to be held in Wyatt's arms. There was zero payoff in getting involved with him. This time, unlike the other times in her life, she'd been warned.

"Alex, you look so far away," Molly was saying.

Alex shook her head. "Sorry. You know me. It takes a few minutes to come down from the clouds and forget work."

What was it that was different about Molly? she wondered, looking more closely at her friend. Something wasn't right there. But when she voiced her concerns to Molly, her friend wrinkled her nose.

"Hey, I'm fine. Serena and Jayne and I are the ones who get to play mother duck to *you* today. Still, I can't believe Wyatt flew us all out here to see you! A private luxury jet. Wow!"

"I know, and I'm still trying to figure out the underlying reason for this trip," Jayne said.

"Wyatt said that you needed people who could help you relax," Serena said. "Alex, what does that mean? What have you been up to that the emergency friend forces have been called in?"

"Emergency friend forces?"

"You better believe it," Serena told her. "I've got the tattoo. Jayne and Molly, too. We'd show you, but then you'd want one, too, and we know you're allergic to needles."

Alex laughed. She relaxed.

"Okay, enough stalling. Spill," Molly ordered.

"There's not much to tell," Alex said, and she related the story of the boy and the ruined papers, the events she had been planning, and eventually the last incident with the angry workmen in the ballroom. No need to mention the latest out-of-control kiss with Wyatt, since she still hadn't wrapped her own mind around what had happened.

"So...what's happening between you and Wyatt?" Serena asked.

"What do you mean?"

"Flying your friends in? That's not one of the usual employee perks."

Of course nothing had been "the usual" between her and Wyatt from the very start.

"He's a very different kind of man," she said carefully.

"Uh-oh," Molly said, and Serena and Jayne nodded.

"Different as in interesting and exciting?" Serena asked.

"Different as in an employer who goes the extra mile for his employees," she said, looking at her friends sternly. "Look, you don't have to worry. I'll be home soon. I called a real estate agent in San Diego, and she's looking for a shop for me to rent."

Because after ending up in Wyatt's embrace the other day what else could she do? The best way to stay smart was to pretend her time here was almost done, plan ahead, get involved in making her dream of a shop a reality. No more dwelling on Wyatt.

"Alex, that's so great—but tell us more about Wyatt," Molly said.

Alex gave her a "stop right there" look. "Nice try, Molly, but I have to tell you I *really* don't want to do this."

"Do what?"

"Answer a lot of questions about Wyatt. I know you're asking because you care, but I really just need to be with you guys today and have fun. Wyatt told me that I wasn't even supposed to utter the word McKendrick's today. I was supposed to be totally lazy and decadent, and that's what I want to be."

"Great! Total decadence works for me," Serena said with a grin.

"Sounds fantastic. So where should we start?" Molly asked.

"Let's start with chocolate, and then double chocolate—maybe triple chocolate—and go from there," Alex said.

"Chocolate what?" Jayne asked.

"Does it matter? It's *chocolate*, Jayne," Serena said.

"Excellent point," Jayne agreed.

So they ate chocolate, and other things a bit higher up the food pyramid. They drank, shopped, and talked nonstop. They tried on clothes they would never wear in public, shoes too high to walk in. And Alex indulged in her secret weakness— wild earrings she bought but could never find a place to wear. They reminisced about incidents in their past and shared private jokes. And if there were moments when the conversation slowed, when Serena looked sad, Molly appeared worried, Jayne seemed heartbroken or Alex drifted away to thoughts of Wyatt, none of them discussed those things. They had this one no-worries-allowed day, and they didn't intend to waste it.

But eventually the day ended. Teary goodbyes were said. Five minutes after all her friends left, Alex got into the limo and turned toward McKendrick's.

As if on cue her thoughts turned to Wyatt. She remembered the sound of his voice, how he had tried to protect her from the view of Jenna and the tourists, how he had promised not to let anyone touch her, how she'd felt when he had kissed her.

Her lips began to tingle, and suddenly the limo seemed to be moving too slowly. She wanted to see Wyatt. She couldn't wait to see Wyatt.

That couldn't be a good thing, and yet when she caught her first glimpse of him, it felt like a very good thing. That tendency to salivate at the sight of him like some Pavlovian puppy was going to be a problem.

If she let it.

Woof, she thought, as she smiled and reached out to take his hands. "Thank you so much for today, Wyatt. It was exactly what I needed."

She rose on her toes and kissed him on the cheek, her silly palm tree earrings dangling. Then she realized that they had an audience. Katrina, the restaurateur who obviously coveted Wyatt, was standing nearby.

* * *

Wyatt read Alex's distress. She hadn't considered the possibility of an audience…although they often had one. That was how she operated: straightforward, nothing held back. She would never consider not offering her thanks or her help if she felt either was needed. It was one of the most appealing things about her, and one that made him insane with worry for her. Someday someone would take advantage of her giving nature. Again. It had better not be him.

"My, aren't we enthusiastic?" Katrina said, in that sultry, snotty way that had never bothered Wyatt before. Maybe because she usually reserved it for people who deserved it. Alex didn't.

He shot Katrina a sheathe-your-claws look. She shrugged.

Then Alex did something he hadn't seen her do before. She straightened her shoulders, emphasizing her full height. She was wearing silly but cute little dangling palm tree earrings that should have looked ridiculous but somehow didn't. Alex was just an inch or so taller than Katrina, but it was enough to give her an edge.

She pulled her shoulders back. Then she looked down her pretty nose and smiled a truly feline smile. "Enthusiastic? I'm *always* enthusiastic, Katrina. You should try it. I hear it's wonderful at preventing age lines."

Ouch! How would Alex know that Katrina was touchy about nearing her thirtieth birthday? This was going to get ugly. He needed to step in before Katrina did some serious damage.

To his surprise, Katrina laughed. "So, the kitten has claws? Touché, Alex. I totally had that coming, but who knew you'd follow through? Interesting. I do appreciate a woman who doesn't back down. Not that we're going to be friends or anything."

Alex blinked. Then she smiled. "Not that we are."

"Nice earrings." It wasn't a compliment.

"I think so." She shook her head, sending the little palm trees dancing.

"So…" Katrina went on. "Wyatt let you have a day off to play while he was here killing himself?"

"That's enough, Katrina," Wyatt cut in. "I don't make my employees work seven days a week."

"I don't know why not. *You* do most of the time."

"I own the place. I get to decide when I work. Now sounds good."

"Is that a not so subtle hint for me to get back to Gendarmes?"

He smiled. "I appreciate the tip about the reviewer coming here tomorrow, Katrina. Thank you."

She returned the smile and turned to Alex. "Since you're going to be only a very temporary fixture here, I guess I can toss you a bone. I *do* like the earrings." And she sauntered out, waving to Wyatt.

When she had gone, Wyatt looked at Alex. She was studying him, a frown line creasing her pretty brows. He was tempted, so very tempted, to gently trace a line right down that frown with his fingertip to get her to smile. The thought caught him off guard. He was not a man given to whimsy.

"What?" he asked.

"You *do* work all the time," she said. "I know you want McKendrick's to show well to the reviewers. I take it that Katrina's got some hint that another one is on the way, and of course that means more hours for *you*. But do *you* ever take time off? Since I've been here you haven't taken a break except for those couple of hours the other day. Weren't you supposed to stay away all day?"

He had been. And he'd come back because she'd been invading his thoughts. "I had something to do," he said.

"Wyatt," she drawled.

"Alex," he drawled back. "Don't worry. I'll take time off."

"When? Don't you ever need to just…kick back? What do you do then?"

Wyatt almost smiled. No one but Alex would ever ask him about "kicking back." As for what he did…suddenly he had another burning desire to show her the Haven. That should have alarmed him. No one even knew he owned it. He'd never taken anyone there. And he never shared secrets with another person. Not Katrina. Not Randy. But…

"What do I do? Come on. I'll take you there."

"There?"

He shrugged, trying to look casual even though he felt anything but. "I have another hotel."

She blinked. "No one ever told me that."

He looked directly into her eyes. "That's because I've never told anyone."

Her eyes widened.

"You don't have to come," he said. And then he realized what this sounded like. A tryst. A man who might be planning on taking advantage of her. "If you're worried, I can tell you that I'm not intending to jump you."

She smiled and shook her head, those little earrings swinging wildly. "I'm not worried. I'm…I'm honored to be your first."

Heat sizzled through him, even though he'd known she had meant that in a completely innocent way. She, however, had obviously finally realized how her words had sounded, and she blushed. Actually blushed. It was charming. *She* was charming. And he burned for her.

"I mean, that I'm honored to be your first visitor. Is it going to be the next McKendrick's?"

He shook his head. "It's definitely nothing like this place. McKendrick's was a sure thing, a prime piece of real estate. The Haven is far less stable," he said, mentioning the property by name for the first time. Trusting Alex.

She gazed directly up into his eyes. "You're not sure you can make it a success."

"Or that I want to try. Failure isn't an option, and it needs…something."

She stood there for a minute, just studying him, as if conducting a computer scan of his thoughts. He'd never had anyone pay that much attention to him, at least not in that way. Women were attracted to his money, his power, maybe even to his looks. But Alex was different. She aimed straight for the core of what made a person tick. He wasn't sure his soul could survive that kind of close examination.

"It's not a very impressive place. You can back out and I won't be offended," he said. But he hoped she would come.

"Why?" she asked. "Why now? Why me?"

He didn't want to examine all the reasons. He didn't want to dig that deep, look inside himself that closely, but he could tell her one true thing. "Because you see possibilities other people miss."

"And if there are no possibilities?"

"I want you to be brutally honest."

She gazed up at him with those soft blue eyes. "I don't like hurting people."

He held her gaze. "You can't hurt me." But he knew he lied.

CHAPTER ELEVEN

ALEX looked at the sad little collection of buildings, and her heart broke for whoever had once tried to make a go of this property and given up. It wasn't near the bustling Las Vegas strip, the cottages were small, parts of the chapel were tumbling down, and yet...

"Beautiful scenery," she said, noticing the stark red rocks in the distance.

"There's that, and also isolation."

She studied the little cluster of buildings, the small attempts at hominess, planters where non-native plants had died long ago, and the remains of an arching trellis outside the little chapel.

Wandering inside the adobe chapel, partially open to the elements where glass was missing from the deep cut-outs of the windows, Alex stood soaking in the atmosphere. It was the most basic of structures, a bare wood floor, plain wood pews with slatted backs. There was no light source. Someone had scribbled graffiti on the big timbers that held up the roof and on the white walls.

Outside there were benches on the path connecting the cottages, their canopy frames empty and skeletal. Everything was silent, deserted, empty.

Alex noticed other little imperfections—the faded blue

door on one cream cottage, a crooked welcome sign over another door, the flowers painted over the entrance to the chapel that would never have occurred naturally in this landscape and yet…

"There's something rather charming and winsome about it," she said.

"You don't have to say that."

"I know."

"Who even *uses* the word *winsome* anymore?"

"I guess I do."

Wyatt smiled. "Winsome it may be. Commercial? Doubtful."

"And yet you bought it."

"I did."

Maddening man. He knew she was looking for an explanation of why a man who owned one of the most successful, state-of-the-art hotels around had purchased this clearly not-likely-to-be-commercially-successful property. In fact, she was willing to bet that of all the properties available at the time that Wyatt bought this, few had been so…sad.

"You'll want to make changes."

He hesitated. "I always make changes. Change is good."

"How long have you had this?"

"A while. More than a year. Almost two."

"And yet…no changes?"

"Not yet. No."

"Why? It can't be lack of funds."

"No. Money isn't a problem."

"So why no changes?"

She waited while he seemed to consider the question. "It has to be right, and yet…I like it how it is, even though I know it's not marketable."

She laughed. "You sound so frustrated with yourself, but

I don't see what the problem is. If you don't need the money, and you like it as it is, why not simply leave it alone?"

"To what purpose?"

"Everything has to have a purpose?"

"Some people think so."

"Do you?"

"Let's just say that I grew up in a world where everything had to have purpose and worth."

She opened her mouth.

He shook his head. "Don't ask me more, Alex. I've already told you more than I've ever told anyone. I don't discuss it."

"You don't like to talk about it because it's painful."

He turned those beautiful wicked green eyes on her. "You are an amazing woman."

"Because I asked you a personal question?"

"No. Because you asked me a personal question about my shady past when I just told you that I don't discuss it."

"It was rude, wasn't it?" And yet she was consumed with the need to know what made Wyatt tick. She was pretty sure that part of that was pain, and her own heart clenched with pain at the very thought. Which should have totally alarmed her.

This was the very kind of thing she had warned herself about a hundred times. She should back away, maintain a distance. Instead, she couldn't seem to stop herself from moving forward.

"Why do you want to know my motives?" he asked, catching her off balance.

"I…I don't know."

But that wasn't strictly true. Wyatt interested her far too much, and feeling even one drop of longing for him could lead her straight to heartbreak. In the past, even with the wrong assumptions she'd made about men, she'd at least had some reasonable chance of success, but with Wyatt that chance was nonexistent. There would never be more than physical attraction on his part. And yet when she looked into those green eyes, and saw that he wasn't as stoic as most people thought, she couldn't help wanting to know everything about him. She couldn't stop herself from feeling things she should be running from.

To her surprise, he chuckled. "You have to be the most straightforward woman I've ever met. Do I refuse to talk about my past because it was painful? Well, it certainly wasn't pretty. My mother didn't like children, and the uncle she left me with liked them even less. He believed in child labor and that a fist was a useful tool in the parenting toolbox. For my part, I was hell on wheels and not the kind of person you'd want to know. As for why I don't discuss my childhood…it doesn't fit the image I've created for myself as owner of McKendrick's. A pathetic story isn't good for a business in a city based on having fun, and since I intend to be successful, I keep my ugly childhood hidden from view."

And yet he had shared some things with her. Twice.

"I hate to lose, but I bought The Haven," he said with a grimace. "She's certainly a sad little establishment, isn't she? Flawed, blemished, imperfect in every way."

Something he had apparently been criticized for by those who should have loved, protected and nourished him. Still, there was affection in his voice.

That was all it took. Alex's protective instincts immediately kicked in. "It's really not a bad little place."

"If you say 'it just needs love,' I'm going to have to laugh. You know that, don't you?"

She wrinkled her nose at him. "It needs attention, and some creativity, and some…some…"

"Don't say it," he warned, and she bopped him on the arm.

"Oops," she said. "That can't be right. You're my boss."

But there was heat in his eyes when she looked up, and she forgot to feel like an employee.

"Alex," he said with a groan. "Don't look at me like that. Don't…"

"Don't what?" she asked on a whisper.

"Don't make me want you."

"I'm not trying to." But *she* wanted *him*.

"You don't have to try. I've wanted you from day one. I should never have hired you."

"Because it's unprofessional?"

"Because I don't want to hurt you, and I might."

"Women want you. You don't want love. It's a given that hearts would be broken."

"I don't want to break yours."

"You won't. I won't let my heart get broken again. I've learned to be strong."

"Then you'd better be strong for both of us, because I'm losing the battle to stay away."

As if to demonstrate, he leaned close, his lips almost touching hers. She felt the zing of electricity arc between them, felt her lips tingle, and heat, and…

She closed the gap. She looped her arms around him and kissed him long and hard and deep.

He groaned. Alex felt faint with longing, with desire, with things she didn't want to face. Reality, she thought. *Go away, reality.*

But reality ignored her, and she had to admit the truth. She wanted to go on kissing Wyatt, to ask him to take her into one of those rickety little buildings and make love with her. And if she did, he would hate himself for hurting her.

And she would break in every way possible. She would be

disgusted with herself for claiming to be strong and then proving that she wasn't.

Wyatt advanced, nibbling at her lips, pulling her against his long, lean, hard body. His arms possessed her; his lips enflamed her. His hands…oh, his hands…

Don't let this happen. As if Jayne or Serena or Molly were there beside her, the voice of reason found her. *You said you were strong*, she thought. *Be strong.*

"Wyatt, I have to stop," she whispered against his mouth, her words garbled.

But, as if her heart instead of her incoherent voice had spoken to him, he released her. Immediately.

"I have to stop doing that," he said.

Alex frowned and crossed her arms. "Do not try to take credit for that one. I gambled. I started it. I ended it. And I told you that I'm strong. I'm capable of controlling things."

As if she'd said something funny, his concerned look turned to a half-smile.

"Don't laugh at me," she commanded.

"I wouldn't think of it. You scare me, Alex."

"I do?"

"Yes. You do." Except his voice wasn't teasing anymore. "I should get you back home."

"Not yet."

He raised one eyebrow, questioning.

"We didn't come here to make love. We came for this sweet little place," Alex said. "And we've ignored her. It's her turn to get some attention, and it's clear that you love her."

He looked at her with those deep green eyes that made her soul ache and yearn. "I don't love anything or anyone."

The cut went deep, although Alex didn't know why. He'd been telling her this from the moment she'd met him. He'd told her in so many words just moments ago. In fact, *everyone* had been telling her that, and why should she be surprised? A man who came into the world subjected to only hate and hitting would have had all the love beaten out of him. But not the caring, she reminded herself. No matter what he said, she'd seen him be gentle with Belinda. He'd done all he could to help Randy. And as for me, Alex thought, he's bent over backwards for me. He cared about some things, on some level.

He cares about these falling-down cottages, she thought. Cottages as imperfect as a beaten boy had once been. So she took a deep breath, took a chance. "I take it you brought me here for an objective opinion. So if I told you to tear it down?"

She could see him swallowing. "You wouldn't do that."

And now she saw why he had kept this place a secret. "You know that most people would tell you to sell it."

"Absolutely. If another person had bought it and I was the one giving the advice, that's what I'd tell them."

"And you're sure I won't do that?"

"I'm reasonably sure of it."

"Why?"

He gave her one of his rare smiles that made her want to curl closer, to rub up against him. "You like to make things better, not tear them down. Randy was snobbish to you, and you looked for the bright side; when Belinda was in labor, you could have shooed the customers away or sent them to Randy, but you made the best of the situation and helped them. It's just not in you, Alex, to throw up your hands and walk away. You see the way things might be. So if you told me to tear this place down, I'd know that it really was completely hopeless."

"I sound like such an idiotic optimist."

He shook his head. "No, you sound like an admirable woman with good ideas."

"But you like winning, and you know that despite my ideas, I don't always win." She hesitated, remembering all the times she had lost. She had tried to win love and ended up shattered. But...what a ridiculous thought. Wyatt was talking about business, not love. She looked up and surprised a concerned look on his face.

"I'm not putting the success or failure of this venture on you, Alex. I'm just asking for your opinion."

"Yet you're a genius in your field. McKendrick's—"

"Was different. The location alone assured its success."

"But you built it into more of a success than other people could."

"Thank you. Let's just say that my odd fascination with the Haven makes it too personal for me to trust my judgment. I don't want it to be personal."

Now at last she saw clearly. "You don't really want to change it, and yet it doesn't fit with your 'change is good, perfection is everything' motto, so you're at a standstill."

"Something like that, yes. I... Maybe I *should* sell it."

With those words Alex knew that this bit of property held a very personal place in his life, even if he didn't want it to. It was a misfit, like he had been, and he was fighting his urge to keep it because only winners were allowed in his life.

Her heart hurt at that thought. She was good at many things, but she had been a loser...so many times.

She took a breath, pushing that thought away. This wasn't about her. It was about Wyatt's battle with his past and what this place represented. What would happen to this place if he sold it? And how would he feel when the deal was done?

She didn't know. She only knew that no matter how rundown the Haven was, it was worth fighting for.

"Don't sell it," she whispered. "It has...real possibilities."

He chuckled. "Such as? You said that as if you weren't sure you believed it."

Okay, the man saw too much. Alex concentrated. Despite her bad luck with men, or maybe because of it, she'd learned to look for the rainbow in the rain. So what was there to work with here?

"How about adding a small, private rustic garden next to each cottage, with native plants and rocks and a viewfinder, so that the visitors staying can see the birds and the local wild-life and get a closer view of the rock formations? It's really a starkly gorgeous area. Or add some charm by placing local history plaques in the cottages. Decorate them with antiques. Maybe enlarge one of the cottages and make it a communal gathering area. Make this a rest-stop for those on their way elsewhere or a place to kick back after days of non-stop activity in Las Vegas. Or..."

"Or what, Alexandra?" Wyatt asked, taking both her hands.

"Or you could just leave it as it is," she said softly. "You don't have to change it at all. You don't even have to rent it out. Imperfect as it may seem to others, it's perfect in its own way if it's what you like."

He reached out and brushed her hair back from her face with one hand. "I knew you'd be good for this place."

His touch was entrancing; his words did wonderful things to her ego, even though she knew he was just being nice. People always teased her about her overeager outlook. Even people who loved her worried that her attitude made her a target for those who wanted to take without giving, and they were right, but...

"What do you think you'll decide to do?"

Wyatt glanced toward the place that clearly called to him. "I'm not sure, but you've given me some springboards. Thank you. I'd better get you back now. We've been gone a long time, and I don't want people wondering what we're doing."

"You think they'll think I've kidnapped the boss?" she teased.

"I think they'll worry that I'm seducing you. Randy is very protective of you these days."

She rolled her eyes. "Randy idolizes you, Wyatt."

"And he knows me. Too well. Randy is grateful to me, but he knows I've got a dark side. And you don't."

"I might have," she said defensively.

He laughed as he helped her into the sleek black convertible and headed back toward McKendrick's. "What have you ever done that was so terrible?" he asked.

She knew, but she didn't want to think about it. Wyatt's concern for her was pushing her over the edge. What had she done that was so terrible? She was very close to falling in love with him. And she certainly couldn't say that.

"I wrote *I heart Erick Swanson* on the bathroom wall at school. In permanent marker. Red, too," she said, feeling silly for saying it. It was the only detention she'd ever received.

Wyatt laughed—a gorgeous, sexy laugh, its tones echoing through the gathering dusk. "Lucky Erick," he said.

"Well, my infatuation didn't last. When word got out, he called me names and made fun of my braces."

"The man deserves to lose all his teeth at an early age," Wyatt said, making Alex smile.

"If only you'd been around in those days," she said. "I would have had a defender."

"You wouldn't have wanted to know me then," he said.

But he was wrong. She wanted to know more of him. She wanted to know all of him.

CHAPTER TWELVE

WYATT had gone back to work with a vengeance, reminding himself of all the reasons he needed to maintain some distance from Alex. A second tier of reviewers had hit McKendrick's. It was clear that the ante was being upped, the city was starting to buzz, and his chief competitor, Champagne, was making great upgrades. They'd had some fantastic reviews. He should be worried. He *was* worried. To come so close and lose would be…difficult, scalding. And yet the competition wasn't what was bothering him the most.

On the way home the other night, he'd asked Alex about her shop, and she'd told him about calling a real estate agent to set things in motion. It was clear that San Diego was her passion. She had major plans. Wyatt identified with that. McKendrick's, Las Vegas…he belonged to this city. But it was equally clear that Alex belonged to San Diego. And also clear that her plans would become a reality in the near future.

He was getting in too deep, flying blind with Alex, with no chance of a future. At least not one that would make her happy.

He needed to remember that this temporary position she was filling was…temporary. Which was a good thing, because Alex was far too clean and pure and joyful for someone like him.

He could tease her and pretend his past was behind him, but he was still the guy whose past colored his present. He dealt in empire building, not love, because needing someone to care and letting that person's opinions matter was impossible. The only safe route was to be an island. Anything else and the risk of someone being damaged was too great. He might not be Erick Swanson, but he could crush Alex just as easily as that idiot had.

If he let himself continue down the path he'd been following. *If* he didn't stop things right now.

He had to stop. No matter how difficult that would be.

Alex was worried. "I don't know what's happening, Jayne, but Wyatt is acting very strange lately," she told her friend during a phone call a few days later.

Silence followed. "Jayne?"

"Strange how?" Jayne's voice had an edge to it. "You sound as if you care about him, Alex…"

"I'm not in love with him. I'm worried, the way I would be about anyone." *Except maybe more*, Alex thought. *A lot more.*

"He probably just has some business issues, Alex. Which isn't your problem. I know you're used to jumping in to help, but you can't save everyone."

"I know," Alex said, and they hung up.

Jayne was right. She was falling into her old routines. Having two fathers turn their backs on her as if she didn't matter had made her too eager to please. That was why she'd helped Robert and Leo and Michael…and why she'd gotten hurt when they'd left her. And now?

The warning bells were clanging, telling her to leave now.

She should. In fact, she'd gotten a call yesterday from her real estate agent. The woman thought something might open up soon. She should be rejoicing at the news. Instead she was thinking about Wyatt.

The other day a male guest had been giving her a hard time, complaining that she wasn't trying hard enough to satisfy his demands. He'd called her an unspeakable name, and she had looked up to see Wyatt, his face fierce as a class-five tornado. He'd come up behind the man, and in a voice so icy that it would have scared Alex had she not known him, given the man ten seconds to vacate the premises.

The man had opened his mouth to argue, but after taking one look at Wyatt's whipcord-lean body and "just try me" expression, he'd headed for the door, mumbling something about intimidation.

"Thank you," she'd said quietly.

"You're an employee of McKendrick's. I take my responsibilities seriously."

Somehow Alex had managed not to flinch at being thus demoted from what had felt like *more* than an employee, but something must have shown in her eyes.

"Don't look like that. I'm doing this for your own good."

"Of course. I *am* your employee."

The low curse hadn't carried far, but Alex had still heard it. "I've tried to tell you not to trust me too far. You were wrong when you said that I could have been your hero during the Erick Swanson incident. I would have been just as bad in my own way, because I would have acted as if you didn't exist."

"Because of the braces?"

"Nothing to do with the braces. I just wasn't...social." His jaw had tensed, his expression had become unreadable, and just like that they were back to being strangers.

Thinking about that pain knifed through Alex. Which was so stupid. She knew the score. Wyatt had walls that couldn't be breached. And yet here she was, making the same mistakes she'd made before, leaping in to help and falling for a man she could never win. The only way to save herself was to walk away. She would.

But not yet. Not yet.

Wyatt walked into the lobby, took one look at Alex and swore beneath his breath. "This is wrong," he muttered to himself.

"What?" Randy's voice came from behind him, catching Wyatt off guard. He hadn't known the man was so near. Still...

Wyatt nodded toward Alex. "She looks tired." Worse, she looked sad. And he was pretty sure that he was to blame. She'd given him her sunshine, and he had ignored her for days. The fact that he was trying to protect her, that he wasn't capable of being right for her, and that he was scared that he was starting to feel things for her that could never be called back was no excuse. She'd held nothing back from him. He'd repaid her with silence and dark moods.

"We all like her, Wyatt," Randy said.

It was a warning. Randy sometimes got away with things that other people couldn't. Maybe because they shared the common bond of a dark past.

"Good. She needs friends here."

"She needs more than that. And she deserves more. She's done more for McKendrick's reputation than anyone but you."

Wyatt turned to look at Randy. The man gave him a sheepish look. "Sorry."

"No. You're right. I've been an ass lately, haven't I?"

"We're all sure that you have good reasons."

"Don't make excuses for me. Being the boss doesn't exempt me from being a human being."

Somehow he kept handling Alex wrong. That would end

soon…because she would leave. But before she left she needed to know that his avoidance of her didn't have a thing to do with her worth. Alex had been a blessing and a gift for McKendrick's. And he hadn't even told her that.

It was past time to tell her a lot of things.

Alex was just leaving work when Wyatt came up to her. "Any chance that you're free tonight?"

She blinked. Wyatt had kept his distance for days. "Is it something about the hotel? Something I need to know…or do?"

He frowned.

"Wyatt?"

His eyes flashed green fire. "I wanted to apologize to you."

She opened her eyes wide. "For…?"

"Being a jerk. Ignoring you. Not acknowledging what you've done for me and McKendrick's." His dark brows beetled.

Alex couldn't help laughing.

"What?" he asked.

"That's the grumpiest apology I've ever received."

"I'm not sure I've ever offered one before."

Her smile blossomed. "Then I'm honored to be the first."

"Are you honored enough to come out with me? Have dinner with me? Let me apologize more…properly?"

The word warred with his tone, and there was absolutely nothing about the look he gave her that was proper.

Her heart began to thud. Tears clogged her throat, but she wouldn't let him see. She had missed him so much, and she was so happy to see him that she didn't care what had brought him back. She wanted to touch him so desperately. All of that combined sent warning signs blaring in her brain. She needed to retreat to safety. To say no.

Her heart lurched and fought her. *To hell with reasonable*

and safe. Her calendar pages were tearing away. Time was running out. And she already knew this was a temporary relationship, headed nowhere, so where was the risk?

"I'd love to have dinner with you."

Had she said that with too much fervor? Wyatt's expression told her he was thinking of more than food, but he smiled gently.

"I'll pick you up at your room in ten minutes."

At her room. The words only made her think how badly she wanted him *inside* her room.

"Casual?" she asked, pretending away that last thought.

"Mmm. I'm bringing a picnic basket from Sparkle."

Alex had never eaten the rooftop restaurant's food, but she had recommended it to many people.

"Wear those cute little palm tree earrings. And shorts. White. A top that's soft. Blue."

She opened her eyes wide. "Is this my boss talking?"

"This is Wyatt the man talking. For this one night let's pretend I'm just a man who knows you'll look amazing in white and blue."

Her heart nearly stopped. Her breath definitely *did* stop.

"Too much?" he asked. "Should I apologize again?"

"No, but if you're not my boss tonight, I'm thinking that you shouldn't expect me to follow every request you give me in my off hours."

"I like it when you use that sassy tone. Have I said that before?" he asked, just before he left to get the food.

No, he hadn't, she thought as she changed clothes. He'd tried to keep everything impersonal, which was probably smart. There was something even more dangerous about this new, friendly Wyatt. She wanted to give him exactly what he'd requested. But that was the mistake she'd made all her life. Trying to win affection by giving people exactly what they wanted. Besides, if she tried too hard he'd know that she was becoming one of those women Randy talked about. Women who ended up with nothing but tears and memories. She did *not* want to be that woman.

When she opened the door to Wyatt a few minutes later, he paused. Then he smiled. "Great shorts, even greater legs, and red definitely looks fantastic on you," he said, referring to her scoop-necked tee shirt. "Maybe even better than blue. And the bicycle earrings are just as good as the palm trees. Good for you for ignoring my arrogant request."

"Thank you." She smiled. "Should we go?"

"Yes. *No.*" She realized that he was looking around her room. Frowning.

"What?"

"Is this really the best I could do for you?"

"Wyatt, this is a gorgeous suite! You moved me in here when I started working for you."

"Yes, but it's just a couple of rooms. There's nothing here that would make it seem like a home. I could have at least made it feel less Spartan."

Alex couldn't help laughing. "Wyatt, I've never stayed in such a plush place before, and you're worrying because I don't have my teddy bear with me, or any reminders of San Diego?"

"Well, I know you love that place. And all you have in here to remind you of home is a picture of you and your friends in my lobby."

"Wyatt, don't worry. I'm fine." She rose on her toes and kissed his cheek. "Come on. I'm starving. Where's the picnic?"

"It's a surprise. You'll see when you get there."

He was right. When Wyatt pulled up in front of the Haven, Alex *was* surprised. There was a new low-profile sign, the native plants in the garden were perfect, and the freshly painted white cottages had blue trim and welcoming little signs above the doors.

She gave a whoop. "Wyatt, you did this so fast!"

"Yes, well, I wanted you to get the chance to see the fruits of your creativity. It's not done yet. I haven't even touched the chapel, and the cottages still need work, but it's a start."

"It's a great start. Can I go inside one of them?"

"Choose your cottage."

That was easy. There was one that was slightly smaller than the others. It was shabbier, with roof work still to be done. It was the underdog, but it looked sound. Alex opened the blue door and stepped inside to find the perfect little cozy nook. The walls had been painted, and the furnishings were plain but pretty oak. The tiny fireplace had been framed in white tiles and timbers, and a fluted jar of desert sand sat on the mantel, surrounded by an arrangement of striking red rocks.

"I thought... The sky-blue pattern in the white upholstery reminded me of..." He looked at her eyes. "Silly, but it seemed to fit."

"Wyatt, it's wonderful. It feels so homey and inviting and comfortable—and I still can't believe you did so much so fast."

"I'd be farther along on this one, too, but I've been doing some of the work myself any chance I get."

Alex widened her eyes. "The great hotelier, engaged in manual labor?"

He shrugged. "When I was growing up I...well, I know a lot about manual labor, Alex."

"I'm not exactly shocked by that."

He gave her one of his rare, full-blown smiles. "I'm beginning to think that nothing much fazes you."

"Yes, well, I've had my moments."

"Those men who used you?"

"They didn't use me. I offered to help them."

"Unlike me, who pretty much waylaid you."

"You didn't waylay me. You bribed me." But she smiled.

"And I'd do it again. You've been magical for McKendrick's," he said.

Why did her heart drop like a rock at that? Because she wanted to be magical for *him*? Randy had warned her that wasn't going to happen.

"You've shared with me, given me more than I ever asked for, and I've given you nothing in return," he said.

Instantly Alex was indignant. "You pay me very well."

"Money is too easy for me. I'm… The truth is, Alex, that I never learned how to be open or giving, but none of that is your fault. Asking you to bend over backward for me, taking all you've given and then shutting you out, wasn't right. The thing is I don't like thinking about my past or talking about it. It was a period of my life when I wasn't strong. My family was, as I've mentioned, dysfunctional. I told you before that I wasn't social. It was partly because I didn't want to take a chance on anyone getting to know me and finding out what went on at my home. Having witnesses would have made things worse."

"You shouldn't have had to live through that."

"And *you* shouldn't have had some idiot of a man take all that you've done for him, fling it in your face and walk away."

He held her gaze. He brushed her palm with his thumb. "I lived through experiences that I hate to remember, but no one ever was able to attack my heart," he said. "Not like that. What kind of a man lets a woman think he cares and then denies her?"

"Some do."

"They're not men. They could have at least said thank you."

She tried to smile.

He swore beneath his breath. "You don't have to be cheerful for my sake. But, Alex, when you leave here I want you to know that there's a man in Las Vegas who'll always be grateful for what you've done for him, and for having the chance to know you for a few weeks."

That was it. Her throat was closing up. Tears were threatening. She didn't want that. Once she started crying, he might know that her feelings ran deeper than his ever would. She could *not* go through that again. Alex took a deep breath and forced calm on herself.

She nodded. "Thank you."

He swore.

"*Thank you*," she repeated, more firmly. "So, how did you go from a life like that to one like this?"

"As soon as I was old enough I ran. I was almost sixteen, and I didn't want to go into the system, so I worked my way around the country. I clawed my way into jobs and saved every penny until I could buy a run-down, falling-down piece of real estate which I fixed up and sold. Then I bought another. My uncle had treated me as a slave at times. Manual labor and the ability to build or repair things was the one thing he gave me that I could use, and I used it. That's all there is to know."

But Alex knew that what he was telling her wasn't half of what he had endured. He had been told over and over that he was worthless. Yet he had somehow educated himself and made McKendrick's into a world-class establishment. And now he continued to work on it and on the Haven, proving over and over again that he had worth. He'd taken a stand in Las Vegas and made the city his own.

That's all there is to know. His words echoed through her

mind. This was as far as they went. It was as much as he was able to give.

"Okay." Her voice came out wrong. He might have thought that revealing his past would keep her safe. Instead she was falling faster and harder than she ever had before.

CHAPTER THIRTEEN

WYATT frowned at Alex.

"What?" she asked.

"Don't look at me that way, Alexandra."

"What way?"

"I'm not sure, but I'm not that boy anymore. I don't need sympathy."

She knew that. What he needed was to be the man he was—strong and commanding. He needed McKendrick's to win the award, to be admired. And he needed to know that he hadn't hurt her.

No man had worried about hurting her before. She wasn't quite sure how to deal with that, so she did it the way she did everything: running on instinct. "Don't worry about me when I'm gone, Wyatt. Those people who hurt me were able to do that because at heart they wanted to be nice. They told lies, trying to offer what they didn't have to give. I believed them, so I felt stupid and cheated when things fell apart. But you don't need to worry about me. That's not what I want from you."

"What *do* you want from me?"

All kinds of things you'll never be able to give me, she thought. "I want honesty, Wyatt, and I've got that. You haven't promised me anything, so you can't be a disappointment."

Something in his eyes shifted, and Alex knew that she'd hit him in a vulnerable spot. That these very words had been used against him at one point. *Darn.* She wished she could go back and rewrite his past, but she couldn't do that any more than she could change her own. So what *could* she do? Where did she and Wyatt go from here…if they went anywhere at all?

We go forward, she thought. *We accept our limitations. He lost the ability to love long ago. I'm scared to believe anyone who offers me love. That should erase any possibility of a complication during the remaining time we spend together.*

A slow, sad smile lifted her lips.

"What's that about?" Wyatt asked.

She couldn't tell him. It sounded too pathetic—making a bid to spend time with him the way so many other women had. And what if he said no? He might easily say no.

"I was just thinking…I'd like to help with this project where I can." *I want to spend more time with you,* she thought.

"You don't have to do that."

"I want to. May I remind you, Wyatt, that I work for you?"

"But this wasn't part of the deal."

"It is now. You asked me to help you think of ways to improve the place. If you thought I would just walk away after that, then you've forgotten about my tendency to butt in."

"I haven't forgotten. It's one of your most endearing qualities." His voice was low, sexy and…

Oh, don't tell me I have endearing qualities, she thought. I'm trying so hard to be practical about you, Wyatt. I don't want to start being impractical again.

"Then I'm butting in. Let me help where I can. Let's get to work," she said, stressing the word *work*.

"Yes, my sassy-tongued boss," he said.

She grinned. "I like being called boss."

This time his smile was full and genuine. "Power goes to your head, does it, Alex?"

"A bit." *But not as much as your kisses, Wyatt.*

Grr. Randy had certainly been right about the power Wyatt held over women. How was she ever going to stop thinking about the man when she went home?

Maybe by remembering that she *was* going home. So as soon as she got back to her desk, she'd find her calendar and cross off all the days she'd neglected to cross off earlier. Soon she wouldn't have to worry about falling in love with Wyatt anymore, because they'd be hundreds of miles apart. Forever.

But not yet. For now she was here, with him. And she wanted...she wanted...

Count, Alex, count, so you can't think about him, she told herself. But then she stopped. *Don't count. Enjoy being with him. Maybe you should even kiss him again.*

If Jayne and Molly and Serena were here they'd help her. They'd try to stop her.

But they weren't here. And Wyatt was. Wyatt, who didn't seem to have ever had much fun or maybe any fun at all in his life when he was growing up. Wyatt who was about work, twenty-four hours a day.

"Watch out, Wyatt," she whispered. "Here I come."

When Alex decided to do something, she did it flat-out, Wyatt realized. Not that he hadn't known that before, but it was even more apparent once they began going to the Haven after hours a couple of times a week. She even argued when he insisted on paying her triple time.

"I chose to do this," she said.

"After I asked for your help."

"But that was only the initial stuff. The 'what should I do

with this place?' stuff. I was the one who made the decision to help with the finishing work."

He stared her down. "This isn't a fight you'll win."

"I wasn't fighting. I was reasoning, Wyatt. *You* were being completely unreasonable."

He smiled.

"What?"

"If you think that calling me names will make me change my mind, give it up, sweetheart. I'm paying you whatever I feel you're worth, and you're worth a lot."

He wasn't just saying that, either. Now that Alex was on board, she kept finding new ways to fine-tune their work. She was at it again today, and the work—and the time—was flying by. Wyatt wanted to slow down, have more time with her.

But he couldn't. Belinda seemed to want to get back to work soon. When that happened, Alex would be going back to the city that held her heart, the source of her dreams.

Something rock-hard lodged in his chest and hurt. Stupid. Alex was sparkling and fun and sexy as hell, but once she was gone he'd forget her quickly. It had always been that way with him and women. There was no reason to believe that things would be different this time. Except for that lodged-rock discomfort when he thought about her going.

"Okay, so we repair what has to be repaired," she was saying. "Then we refinish the floors, but not so they look new. Just so they look a bit weathered and worn down by love."

He couldn't help smiling.

"What?"

She had one hand on her hip and an indignant tilt to her head that made him want to walk right over to her, slip his fingers into her silky hair and cover her mouth with his own. But he held back.

"Are we going to put 'weathered by love' on the brochure?" he asked.

"You'd think that was funny, wouldn't you? But…well, it would at least be true. You love this place, and you're sort of weathering it, with your tools." She groaned. "Forget I even suggested that. We'll worry about the brochure later when we— I mean, when *you* start renting these out."

That solemn reminder that there needed to be an end to all this sent them both back to their tasks. Alex cleaned. He sanded. She decorated. He repaired. He could easily have hired someone else to do these tasks, but Alex was the only person he wanted here, and she seemed to understand.

"You know what I like best about this place?" she asked.

He turned and waited.

"It's not too perfect. It's homey, cozy."

"Small," he said.

"Hey, don't criticize the Haven," she told him.

"I'm still not sure why I'm doing this. No one's going to want to come here. There's none of the glitz of Las Vegas, and it's not rustic enough for outdoor types."

"You're doing it because you want to," she said simply. "Because it gives you pleasure. For fun. Aren't you?"

Wyatt looked at Alex, dressed in a pair of white shorts and a blue tank top. His favorite, he thought with a smile. Although wasn't anything she wore his favorite? Right now she was barefoot, and stretching up on her toes to hang a picture of the desert rocks on the wall. What a lovely picture *she* made.

"I'm having fun," he agreed, as she glanced over her shoulder.

"I could show you some real fun," she said, and he raised a brow.

To his surprise, his sassy Alex looked self-conscious. She squirmed. "I didn't mean it that way, although…that *would* be fun. I'm talking about kid stuff—goofing off, messing around, doing things just for sheer joy."

"I know what fun is, Alex."

"You know, I'm not sure I believe you."

"Fun is for my guests."

"Maybe you need to demonstrate the basics for them."

"Nice try, Alex. But I have work to do."

Now she was frowning, and not in a teasing way.

"I promised myself I wouldn't even allude to this, but didn't you ever have a chance to goof off when you were a kid?"

He sighed and put down the wrench. "I shouldn't have shared that stuff with you. Now you're pitying me."

"You have got to be kidding. You own and run McKendrick's. You hobnob with the big boys. You're admired and envied. But that's all work on some level. None of it spells play. You need a how-to-kick-back tutor, and I'm just the person for the job. Come on." She pivoted on her heel, grabbed a pair of sandals, took Wyatt's hand and headed for the door.

"Mind if you tell me where we're going?"

"I'd rather not. But I'll tell you this—I'm off the clock right now."

The next thing Wyatt knew he was standing in a huge room with blue carpeting and what looked like a million pinball machines.

"Now, we just need some tokens," Alex was saying. "Then I'm going to beat you at pinball. No mercy. I'm very good at this." And she wrinkled her nose and smiled at him.

Two men standing nearby pounding the flippers on a game turned and stared at her, their tongues practically hanging out of their mouths. Wyatt wanted to throw his body over her. No, he wanted to wrap her up in his arms. But first he had to catch her. She was bouncing down the aisle, headed for a machine with a half-naked woman on the screen and lots of bells and whistles, apparently, because Alex licked her lips in anticipation.

Wyatt groaned.

"Don't worry. I promise that this will be fun and it won't hurt a bit," Alex said.

The woman didn't know what she was talking about. Every muscle in his body was taut. He ached to touch *her*, not a machine. But, darn it, she was clearly excited about teaching him all about this stuff, so he was going to have fun or die trying.

And then he was going to kiss her. More than once.

Wyatt knew that Alex had intended this trip to the Pinball Hall of Fame as a way to get him to have fun playing games, and he was, but he was having a lot more fun just watching Alex.

"Yes!" she said as she flipped the flippers and saved the little steel ball from a close call with doom.

Her slender, nimble fingers were lightning-quick as she made the ball fly up ramps, light up lights and hit targets, giving her extra points. The quick caress of those fingers sent heat swirling through Wyatt, and he did his best to tame the way she affected him. Her hips and sometimes her whole body rocked as she threw herself into the fray, while still managing to negotiate the game without causing the dreaded tilt light to come on. And when the satisfying knocking sound indicated that she had racked up enough points to win a free game, she took her eyes off the game long enough to flash him a million-dollar smile.

"Impressive," he said.

"Thank you. Now it's your turn." She stepped aside.

"I've never done this before," he said, feeling sheepishly like a virgin…which he hadn't been for a great many years.

"You've never played pinball? How can that be?"

"No time. And, of course, I didn't know any enthusiasts like you."

She shrugged. "There was an old machine in a hamburger shop I used to hang around when I was a teenager. I caught the bug. Of course, machines are hard to find anymore. They've been replaced by other types of games, computers and home game systems. This place is not only huge, it's one of a kind, run as a nonprofit by a man who donates any excess money to charity, so it's doubly awesome in my opinion. Come on. I'm going to show you what pinball heaven is like."

Wyatt laughed. "Heaven, Alex?"

"We all have our little fantasies, Wyatt."

So true. His current fantasies all revolved around Alex, and if her weakness was playing a game that involved keeping a stainless steel ball from rolling off the low end of a steeply slanted plane, he was willing to do his best to make her happy.

Within minutes he had caught her fever. Wyatt didn't know if it was the game, or the woman who was cheering at his side and practically wriggling with joy when he did well, but he gave his all to keeping that ball in play. He didn't even know how much time was passing. He was probably neglecting some important something happening at the hotel, but his attention was totally focused on the moment, the thrill of competition, the woman who seemed to forget everything but this time, this event.

"That was amazing, the way you did that, Wyatt. For a few nail-biting seconds there, I thought you were going to lose it, but the way you kept the ball in play for so long was totally amazing. And you won *two* games on one quarter."

Wyatt glanced down at Alex and saw that she was practically dancing on her toes, laughing up at him, totally caught up in the sheer excitement of doing something silly but challenging.

"You're so easy to entertain," he teased.

"I am so *not* easy." She pretended to pout, but then her turn came, and she was back to bouncing around and entertaining him all over again.

The truth was that winning a game wasn't all that amazing. He'd done a lot more notable things. He'd spent years trying to prove that he had worth, to erase all traces of what had been told him and done to him as a child, and he had proved himself many times over. But this moment, this woman, who was so spontaneous and transparent in her joy, made him feel as if he'd won a race, climbed a difficult mountain. He felt carefree, released from the constant push to do well. Maybe because he was pretty darn certain that even if he had let that ball slip away Alex would have still smiled at him.

When his turn came again, he did just that. On purpose. He looked at Alex, who was staring at him, suspicion in her eyes.

"Did you let that slide by without even trying?" she asked.

"I might have."

"Oh," she said. "You must be sick of this, humoring me. I forget that not everyone likes pinball, and I've probably kept you here too long. How rude of me not to even notice that you weren't enjoying yourself."

He caught her hand. "Alex, I'm having the time of my life. I just…I just couldn't seem to save that ball." If it took lying to bring her smile back, he was more than willing to lie.

It worked, and then some. She smiled. She reached up and placed her palm on his jaw, sending heat in a rush through his whole body. "It would have been a difficult save for anyone," she said. "You made a valiant effort."

Obviously she was willing to lie, too.

But eventually it was time to get back to reality and the hotel. He insisted on walking her to her room again. But when she opened her door, and he stood waiting for her to enter, he was reminded again of how wrong this room was for her.

"What?" she said when he frowned.

"It doesn't even *look* like you. Your desk downstairs is…"

"A mess?" she asked with a laugh.

"Yes, but you've put lots of…interesting things on it."

"They're just silly little Las Vegas things. A replica of the Eiffel Tower, a homemade McKendrick's snowglobe from a customer, a picture of that first tour group."

What would she have in her room if she weren't here temporarily? If she were at home?

"Do you miss San Diego?" he asked suddenly. He couldn't believe he'd never asked her that.

She thought about it for a second. "I miss my friends, and sure, everyone misses their home when they're away. With my background I probably have a tendency to cling to an actual physical place more than most people do. But Las Vegas has been exciting, and it's beautiful and enticing and…"

He thought about the fact that she hadn't had a real home growing up. And that a hotel was not a home.

And that he couldn't tell her how he felt when he would send her away, anyway. How could he do that to her when she'd already told him about all those people who had pretended they wanted to stay with her and then sent her on her way?

She looked at him. "This…this whole experience has been very exciting."

Has been, she had said. As if she were already thinking ahead to the time when she would be gone. She missed home and all those significant places, and he hadn't even known that, hadn't even thought of it.

"Do you have interesting things in *your* room?" she asked suddenly. "Reminders of favorite places or events?"

He gave her a stern look. "I don't spend much time there."

She blinked at that. "Not even when you... I mean, when you sleep?"

He knew what she had been going to say. She was wondering where he took the women he dated. "I don't bring women to my room. It would be noted by someone on the staff. It might be misconstrued."

"People might start making bets on when you were going to marry. Or break a heart," she said solemnly.

"I know about those bets. I don't approve of them."

"The employees don't mean any harm. They admire you, and they're interested in what you do."

"I know, but someone could get hurt."

"Me?" she asked suddenly. "You're talking about me? I don't let those bets bother me. It's not as if there's ever going to be an outcome, anyway. You and I aren't...doing anything."

That was it. All this talk of who he slept with and where he slept, when all he could think about was making love to Alex...

Wyatt swept her into his arms. She came willingly, easily, fitting against his body so perfectly.

"Don't let me do something stupid and harm you in some way," he said.

"I won't. I promise. Neither of us wants forever. Now, shut up and kiss me, Wyatt. I want you to kiss me."

He claimed her lips, tasted her, touched her. He swept his hands up her sides, over the curve of her hips and up beneath the soft cloth of her shirt to the even softer flesh beneath. She was exquisite, warm.

"Don't stop touching me, Wyatt," she said. She pressed her palms against his shirt, slipped a button from its mooring and slid one hand inside.

His knees nearly buckled and he turned, leaning against the wall, pulling her against his heart as he kissed her again.

But from this position, he was very aware that they were in a public hallway. Alex must be even more aware. If she opened her eyes, the wall would only be inches from her face. And if a member of his staff came down the hall, *he* wouldn't suffer. No one would think anything of it, but as for Alex…

"Open your eyes, Alex," he whispered against her throat as he kissed her there, then kissed her lips, breathing in the sweet jasmine scent of her one last time.

"Wyatt?" she said, opening her eyes. Somewhere in the distance an elevator bell dinged. She groaned. "Did I really ask you to not stop touching me?"

"Don't even consider looking guilty. It did incredible things for my ego."

She shook her head and gave him a sad smile. "As if your ego needed stroking. If anyone knew we were here, women would be lined up for the chance to knock me aside and take my place."

"I could easily say the same thing about you."

"That men would be lining up to kiss me? Wyatt, don't be silly. I mean, there might be a few, but…"

"Alex." He pulled her to him in one swift move, gave her a hard, passion-filled kiss and then forced himself to let her go. "I'm telling you there would be hundreds, and I get the last word here, so don't argue."

He looked down and could see that she was fidgeting. "Are you counting?" he asked.

"No, I'm kissing," she said, rising on her toes to give him an equally passionate kiss. "Then I'm leaving before I do something we'll both regret, like dragging you into my room."

And she hastily retreated behind her door. Just before she

shut it completely, she glanced through the small opening at him. "Wyatt?"

He waited.

"I *was* counting. It didn't work."

She closed the door and left him standing there, wanting her.

He was never going to be able to sleep tonight. So he wouldn't. Yet. First he had something very important to do.

CHAPTER FOURTEEN

WHEN Alex got off work the next day, she went to her room to change and found a box on the table. A note from the maid read: "Mr. McKendrick said this arrived today."

How odd. She'd had her mail forwarded since coming here, but Wyatt had had nothing to do with that.

Opening the box, she peeked inside. Nestled beneath layers of packing plastic and tissue paper was a delicate and exquisite mini pearl ceramic version of the California Tower in Balboa Park. There was also a gorgeous painting of the San Diego-Coronado Bay Bridge, a soft yellow and white pillow with the words *San Diego Your Way* embroidered on it, and a complete set of photos of the day she and Jayne, Molly and Serena had taken a harbor cruise. No serious faces had been allowed in those photos, and they made Alex smile. In addition there was a collection of her favorite CDs and DVDs, a pretty box filled with her favorite mints, and a blue basket with a package of citrus-scented potpourri similar to one she kept at home.

She breathed in the wonderful scent and looked in the box. No note, no anything. But those photos…

Alex frowned and instantly texted her friends.

Setting up video conference call. 8:30 tonight. Need to talk to all of you. Need to see you.

While she waited, she tried not to think about the most likely source of her plunder. It was too coincidental for Wyatt to have twice berated himself for the standard hotel décor of her room and then have this treasure box appear.

Eight-thirty rolled around and she had all three of her friends' faces visible on the screen. Molly looked worried. "Something's wrong, isn't it?"

Instantly Alex felt contrite. "I guess calling a video conference with less than an hour's notice *was* a bit extreme. No, sweetie, nothing's wrong. Well, not flame or hurricane wrong. I just… How did I end up with photos of our harbor cruise outing? They were in a box of things the maid left in my room, and naturally only you three have those pictures, and…"

Jayne sighed. "I knew we should have told you about Wyatt's phone call, but he asked us not to."

"You talked to Wyatt?"

"Jayne talked to Wyatt," Serena said. "He was worried that you didn't have any personal reminders of home and that you were stuck in Las Vegas without friends."

"He wanted us to tell him what types of things you liked to have around you," Molly added.

"So we put our heads together and gave him some suggestions and— Are you all right?" Jayne asked. "Why would Wyatt decide this now, after you've already been there several weeks?"

Do not tell them that he was in your room. Just don't, Alex ordered herself. Then she sighed. These were her *best* friends.

"He hadn't seen the inside of my room until a couple of days ago," she said with a sigh.

"And now he has." Serena made the obvious conclusion, getting it out in the open. "Alex, what aren't you telling us?"

That I'm getting in over my head. That I'm in danger of losing the bet. "He's a great person, a great boss, and, okay, his kisses exceed even my wildest fantasies. But you're absolutely *not* to worry. I'll be home soon, and when I get there I'll be fine. In fact, I'll be wonderful. I'll have enough money to rent a store and begin on the dream I've had for years. My real estate agent tells me that she might have a lead."

"O...kay," Jayne said. "But somehow most of that doesn't reassure me."

Uh-oh. She needed to try again. But Alex took one more look at the contents of the box and her throat began to close up. She knew she couldn't do a better job of reassuring them when she was, in fact, teetering on the edge of disaster.

"Sorry, but I had to tell you how much I love all the things."

"We haven't seen them. Tell us what was in the box," Serena coaxed.

Alex explained. "You sent the photos, though, didn't you?"

"Jayne had them. We should have been the ones to do what Wyatt did," Molly said.

"Why? I could have fixed my room anytime." But she hadn't. Why? She shook off the question. "Anyway, I'm glad I have the photos. So...how are all of you doing?"

There was a hesitation.

"I'm coping," Jayne said.

"I'm fine," Molly added.

"Things are...moving along," Serena said.

Somehow none of that sounded any more convincing than her own protestations, Alex thought. She wondered how much of her friends' current uneasy situations could be traced back to that initial weekend here in Las Vegas.

Not that it mattered. Once you'd opened a box you could never go back and pretend you didn't know what was inside. And you couldn't undo a Las Vegas weekend.

She looked at the spilled-out contents of the box from Wyatt, and her heart twisted. She realized just why she hadn't done anything with this room before. If she'd settled in too much, if she'd allowed herself to nest and build a place here, she might have started allowing herself to dream that she belonged to and with Wyatt. She didn't, and she never would.

And to do her work and do it well, she had to just put that out of her mind. If Wyatt ever thought he'd hurt her, the guilt would haunt him. And he already had too many ghosts to battle.

She had to guard her heart in order to guard his. But in the middle of the night her dreams were haunted by the memory of Wyatt's strong arms around her. And in the morning she woke up clutching the yellow pillow, damp with her tears.

Angry at herself, she went straight to her desk, pulled out her calendar and marked off more days. Two extra days, in fact, which made no sense, but the mere act of crossing things out made her feel stronger.

How was she ever going to survive these next few weeks? *I'll find a way*, she promised herself. *I'll be strong. I won't love Wyatt…unless I already do.*

Wyatt was making plans. He'd just received word that the last round of reviewers, the most exacting reviewers, would be descending on the hotels in question this week. They would be examining everything with white gloves and magnifying glasses, including the proprietors. In this final round he had a crucial part to play, but he was ready. He welcomed the challenge.

Thanks to his staff and Alex, McKendrick's was ready, too. The ballroom, rechristened several times but currently known as La Dance had been finished, and Alex's weekly dances were being held there. There were also self-defense classes, of course, and she'd set up a movable feast wherein guests traveled from one restaurant to the next for different courses. Her latest was a Saturday midnight aquatic perform-ance that was drawing guests almost as much as the dances and restaurants. But of course the owner of Champagne also had his hotel in top form. And things could always go wrong...

He would make sure they went right for McKendrick's. The culminating event of his career was at hand, and he in-tended to win, to crush the past with success.

But he had barely had that thought when he received another phone call. "Wyatt?"

It was Alex. Calling him. And she sounded...not like Alex.

"On my way," he told her, hanging up the phone and rush-ing out to her desk. When he got there, she was standing, shaking her head.

"I didn't mean for you to come. I just..." She looked down at her telephone. One of the lights was flashing. "I got a call from my real estate agent in San Diego. I didn't know what to tell her."

Something inside him started to crumble. "Bad news?" She wasn't smiling.

She shook her head, her pretty hair sliding across her cheek. "No. Good. She's found a place for me."

Crumbling was too tame a word for what was taking place inside him. She was going, and he wasn't ready.

"But I have to go look at it right away. Now. The price is low enough that she thinks someone else will snatch it up if I don't get there today."

"Then you'll go."

"I don't like to desert my post."

And he didn't want to lose even an hour with her, but…

"Alex, I know real estate like I know this hotel. I've played this game before and mostly won, but I've lost once or twice, too. When it means this much, you *have* to go and check things out, make sure they're right, examine every detail of the property, the neighborhood, the lease. You have to jump if the real estate agent is right and jumping is what's required."

Those big blue eyes widened. She took a deep, visible breath. "Okay. I will. This is…I didn't expect this so soon. I confess that I'm a little unsettled. I wonder…would you mind…that is, I've done my homework, and I'm pretty sure I know how to cover the bases and ask the right questions about the shop, but just in case I forget something, could you write down the most important things I need to find out? You know how I rely on notes."

Wyatt wanted to take her right into his arms. All she'd ever wanted was a home. Someday she would have a real one. Just because she'd met some losers, some takers, it didn't mean every man would be like that. Sooner or later the right man would arrive on a white horse, loving every lovable thing about her. That guy would stay and give her a real home.

But until that white knight came along, this shop would be her home, her haven, the thing she threw her heart and soul into. It had to be right. He wanted it to be perfect for her. And because of that…

Wyatt knew what he knew. Real estate agents were useful and necessary, but negotiating a winning business site could be a shark fest. Location and setup would determine whether Alex's business would succeed or become a statistic, one of the huge number of small businesses that failed every year. Failing would crush her spirit.

Wyatt's gut wrenched, but he forced himself to smile. Alex was still waiting for his response, her eyes filled with uncertainty.

"Real estate negotiations are my specialty. I want to accompany you," he said.

And if the reviewers came while he was away? He'd been planning for them, working toward this award and this validation forever. Being named "the best"…how much did he crave that? This was the culmination of everything he'd been heading for since the day he'd run from the people who had nearly buried him with abuse. He wanted it like parched earth wanted water, but…

Alex. She'd spent a lifetime having the chair kicked out from under her. Love stolen. Pride mangled. Her heart battered. She'd fought to reclaim herself, and this business was to be her prize, her salvation.

"*Let* me accompany you," he clarified.

If the reviewers came… Well, this was Vegas. Sometimes a man had to gamble. The odds were pretty good that they wouldn't come today. That was a good thing, because telling Randy or any of the others about the final review wasn't an option. Someone would leak the news to Alex. She might insist on negotiating her deal alone. No backup. No support. Gambling for her happiness without all the tools in the real estate toolbox.

"Alex?" he said.

The hotel would wait. He was not going to sacrifice Alex's chance of success to McKendrick's. Because no matter how much the hotel and the award meant to him, she came first. And he wasn't even going to allow himself to *think* about what that meant or how stupid he was for feeling that way. In the end, even if McKendrick's won, he was going to lose.

He'd be damned if she lost, too.

"Are you sure?" The hopeful look in her eyes sealed the deal.

"Absolutely positive."

"I would so love to have you with me," she said, sending heat and ridiculous hope rocketing through him.

Alex was worth more than McKendrick's, he thought again. It was practically blasphemy. But it was the truth.

"Then let's make this happen." He took her hand…maybe for one of the last times ever.

Alex looked at Wyatt. They were in a nice but not terribly exclusive part of San Diego. "What do you think?" she asked, but what she really wanted to ask was *What are you feeling? What will life be like when I'm here all the time and you're not with me?*

This shop was what she'd been wanting for so long that she should have been exultant. Instead, all she could think about was Wyatt.

"I'd like a report on all the properties in this area and what they've gone for during the past two years," he was telling her real estate agents. "Also some community information. Incidents of petty theft and any other criminal activity in the area."

Alex blinked. "Criminal activity?"

He smiled. "Every area has some. It's good to be informed both from a practical and an insurance perspective. Plus…I want you safe."

"I should have thought to ask that."

"You would have. You know what you're doing. But when a transaction is personal and emotions are involved, it doesn't hurt to have a…a friend along."

Alex's head was spinning. She *did* know most of the questions to ask, but they seemed strangely unimportant right now.

They were being overshadowed by her feelings for Wyatt, the knowledge that her time with him really was ending. And he had called her a friend. Her heart plummeted. She'd done it again, hadn't she? Fallen in love with a man she'd tried to help. Done something stupid. Because, even though for the first time ever a man was helping *her*, the end result would be the same as before.

No, not the same. Far worse. What she was feeling for Wyatt was so much more intense and— No, she couldn't let herself become emotional. Wyatt would key in on that and be worried. So Alex took a deep breath. She looked down at her list of questions.

"About the security deposit…" she began, just as the real estate agent's telephone rang. The woman picked it up.

"It's for you," she told Wyatt, and Alex remembered Wyatt turning off his phone when they entered the office. He frowned, but he took the phone.

"McKendrick," he said.

The voice on the other end of the line was loud enough that Alex could tell it was Randy. He was clearly upset.

Wyatt frowned some more. He took a visible breath and ran his hand through his hair. "It won't be quick. We have a few things to finish up here. I've got the Cessna but…she's busy. Hold the fort."

Before Alex could say a word, he handed the phone back to the agent. He wasn't smiling, but Alex could tell that he was simply going to go back to what they'd been doing.

"Wait," she said. "What did Randy want? I assume I'm the 'she' in 'she's busy'?"

Wyatt shook his head. "There are just some reviewers there. He's a little nervous."

Alex blinked. "Wyatt, are these the *final* reviewers?"

"They might be."

"They'll expect to meet you. Those are the rules for the final round."

"And that's *not* happening. Your real estate agent is right. This property is a prize, and this deal needs to be finalized today." He firmed his jaw and turned away.

Alex couldn't believe what she was hearing. "Wyatt, what's going on? Don't you want to win? This is your everything."

Now he turned back. He looked into her eyes. "And this is *your* everything. I've had years to work on my dreams. Now it's your turn to have yours come true. I want to make sure that it actually happens and that you have no regrets."

Oh, but she was going to have regrets, no matter what happened with this shop. She was never going to have Wyatt. "You're sacrificing yourself."

"I'm doing what's right."

"And so am I." She pulled her cell phone from her purse.

"What are you doing?"

"I'm helping you."

"Not this time. This time you're the one who gets to win."

Her heart clenched. Her throat clogged with tears. Real tears threatened to fall, and she was afraid she wouldn't be able to stop them. What could she say? How could she fix this? All her years of fixing and helping had never prepared her for this.

Alex searched her brain for whatever she could say to make him see reason. She struggled and prayed and cursed stubborn men who didn't know what was best for them. Finally she resorted to her last resort idea.

"Wyatt, how do you think I'll feel if you don't win this?" she asked. "I've worked hard for this award, too. I've given it all I have and all I am. I've stayed up nights trying to think of ideas that will give the hotel an edge. If McKendrick's loses, it won't be just your loss. It will be mine, too. I *need* you to win."

She hated using guilt on him, and she cursed herself for doing something so low, but darn it, he was going to sacrifice something that meant winning out over those jerks who had raised him. All because she had told him that if she didn't get this property today, she would lose it.

"Wyatt, this property is nice, but San Diego is a big, gorgeous city. Lots of property coming and going." She didn't have a clue if what she was saying was true. She was totally flying by the seat of her pants. "There will be other shops. Better shops." She held up her hand to keep her real estate agent quiet.

Wyatt hesitated. Was he going to dig in and get stubborn on her, withdraw from her? His jaw tightened. Alex panicked.

"Wyatt, please," she whispered.

At her words, his green eyes flashed fire.

"All right. We'll try. And you're right that there'll be better shops. I intend to see that you get the very best. But, Alex, don't get your hopes up about us getting back in time to make a difference. The reviewers are at the hotel now, and we're not in Las Vegas."

"But it's not that far by air. You have your Cessna, and I can practically see the airport from here. What you need is someone to stall, and *not* just Randy alone," she said. "I love him, but he cares too much not to be nervous. You need people who know how to work a room. You need friends, people who care about you, Wyatt."

Was that a mutinous look in his eyes? It was. She knew it so well. She loved it so well. But…

"You know I'm not that guy," he said.

"You *are*. You just don't want to admit it. Look what you've done for me. You just told me that you were a friend, coming with me. That makes *me* your friend." Even though it hurt like heck to think the man she loved was only her friend. "And there's…there's Katrina. She really *is* a friend. She told you about that reviewer before, and she has employees who can manage the restaurant when she's not there. And those two ladies that first day I was there—Joanne and Meredith. They come back all the time. Part of the reason is you. And I know you've gotten e-mails from the mother of that little boy you helped."

"You're pushing it, Alex."

"How about Beverly from the clothing store? She adores you. If she could slip away to help, I'll bet she would. And Harold, too."

"They're business people."

"Who like you and respect you," she said, crossing her arms. "And if you'd just let them, they'd be your friends. I know these things. I may not have all the answers where real estate is concerned, but I know friendship. You can stall for time, Wyatt. If you hurry. Katrina will come in and schmooze those guys. She'll feed them. Randy will give them whatever extras you tell him to give them. And I'll coach Jenna. She can be quite engaging with a little encouragement."

For the first time ever Wyatt looked uncertain.

"Wyatt," she drawled, "please try this. Think of all your other employees at McKendrick's who've worked so hard for this. McKendrick's is in their blood." That was low, it was sneaky, but she no longer felt guilty.

"You're a vixen," he said.

She held out her phone.

"Thank you, but I've got most of those numbers on mine. For professional reasons," he said.

But his hands, always strong, always capable and sure,

shook a little as he dialed. Alex had never loved him so much or been so proud to know him.

His voice was somewhat stilted as he humbled himself, opened himself and asked for favors. But he did ask.

"We'll be in touch," he told the real estate agent as he grabbed Alex's hand. Then he smiled down at Alex.

Her heart somersaulted as he took her hand and they sprinted toward the door.

CHAPTER FIFTEEN

WHEN Wyatt and Alex walked into McKendrick's, he had no idea what to expect. The calls he'd made earlier had been uncomfortable. He was used to giving instructions to employees, asking fellow businesspeople to work with him—but to ask a personal favor, something purely for himself? He'd barely been able to get the words out. Only Alex sitting there nearly in tears over the situation, and the fact that she had reminded him that she and the other employees had slaved for this award had enabled him to ask for what he needed.

So when they came through the revolving doors into a lobby that was filled with light and music and the sound of hearty laughter, Wyatt nearly stopped short.

To some extent things looked as they usually did. Randy was at his station waiting on customers with his normal patience and professionalism. All the usual activities of a hotel lobby were taking place.

But over on one of the corner sofas, Katrina was entertaining a well-dressed portly balding man, who was leaning in to listen to a story she was telling.

Seth, the waiter, was serving hors d'oeuvres and drinks to Beverly and Harold. They were deep in conversation with an elegantly coifed woman who was telling some sort of story.

To his surprise, timid, nervous Jenna was seated at the baby grand piano that seldom got used. Denny was seated next to her on the bench, and she was smiling as she played. Denny's mother, baby in arms, was singing in a clear, strong voice that no one would ever have expected from such an ordinary-looking woman. Joanne and Meredith were harmonizing with her. Other employees were doing simple tasks—filling water pitchers, answering guests' questions—all looking perfectly calm and happy. As if there weren't two major reviewers taking in every single word, action, note.

To his surprise, Belinda, not Lois, was at the concierge desk. She smiled and waved at him. "Alex?" he said.

"Yes. I called Belinda. Lois needed to go home, and I thought Belinda might be willing."

Which made his heart lurch. With Belinda on her way back, Alex would be leaving. But he couldn't let his feelings show. She was responsible for the miracle taking place in this room, and he would be damned if he let her down.

"Showtime, sweetheart," he said.

She gave him a quick glance, but then she pasted on a smile and moved forward with him. To his surprise, the portly man got up and moved toward him with a big grin on his face. "Did she get it?"

Wyatt blinked.

"The shop, man. Katrina here tells me that you take so much interest in your employees that you volunteered to help your young concierge with her real estate transaction. Did she get it?"

"Yes. It's perfect. And I couldn't have done it without Wyatt," Alex lied.

"I have to say, Mr. McKendrick," the elegant woman said, rising to her feet, "you've developed wonderful community relationships. That all these people should have come out to make sure things were running smoothly so you could attend to this young woman's affairs is, frankly, rather amazing. Especially when some of them have businesses of their own to run. And your employees seem unusually happy in their work. Do you… I mean…how do you manage that? Is it real, I wonder?"

"Mr. McKendrick would *never* use coercion. He leads by example," Jenna said suddenly, then clapped her hand over her mouth, her cheeks turning pink.

The woman laughed. "I won't mark him down for that remark," she promised, and then she and the man asked Wyatt if he could give them a personal tour and answer some questions.

His employees and, yes, his friends, had worked their magic.

"Wish me luck!" he told them, with a big smile.

A cheer went up from the room as he led the reviewers away from the lobby. Some time later, after a less friendly and very businesslike interview, he and the reviewers returned to the lobby. To his surprise everyone was still there. Pretending they were busy.

The balding man, Bob Zane, smiled. "Loyal, I see," he said.

"I can't wait to see what your competitor can show us," the woman, Arlene Rogers added. She held out her hand to Wyatt.

Wyatt shook each of the reviewers' hands. "I'm sure you'll find a lot to like. Mark Whittington is a fine businessman, with some great ideas, and Champagne is an impressive hotel."

"Does he lead by example, too?" Arlene asked.

"I have no idea. What I do know is that I have the finest employees, the best professional contacts and some of the greatest friends in Las Vegas. My thanks to all of you for holding the fort until I could make it here," he said to the room at large.

"It's been a pleasure meeting you, Mr. McKendrick," Bob Zane said, and the woman murmured her agreement.

When they had gone, Alex leaned in next to him. "You'd better go say a few words to Katrina and all the others."

"Yes, they went out of their way for me, thanks to you."

"No. Thanks to *you*. You called your friends. They answered the call. That means I think you're going to win in more ways than one," she said, and then she slipped away to talk to Belinda.

Wyatt watched her go. This should have been an exultant moment. It was in many ways. But in one crucial way Alex was wrong. He would lose her, and there was no way to stop that from happening. Asking her to stay wouldn't be fair. Then he would just be one of those guys she'd already known. The takers who stole her dreams.

Instead he turned toward his friends. The first friends he'd ever had, the ones he would never even have known about if not for Alex.

It had been a long day, an interminable day, Alex thought, watching Wyatt escort Beverly, the last of their visitors, to the door. He looked taller and stronger tonight, but not happier.

A pain zipped through her heart. She loved him, and she would spend her life wondering what he was doing, if he was happy. Because, shop or no shop, she had to leave him. Her time here was done. There was nothing here for her.

Especially not Wyatt. She needed to start forgetting him right away, try to start healing her heart, and yet she couldn't help wondering why he didn't look totally happy after the way things had played out here. She had a hunch she knew why.

She walked up to him. "You're not worrying about the fact that I let the shop slip away, are you?" she asked. "You don't feel responsible in any way? Because you aren't. That was my choice, and I meant what I said. I'll find something else."

He smiled down at her. "You can stop the cheering section

now. I'm not fragile. No, I'm not happy that we didn't have time to seal the deal. I'm determined to make it up to you, to get you that shop, but mostly I'm grateful to you. You really helped me out here."

He gave her a full green-eyed smile. Devastating stuff. But his words…she'd heard those words before, seen that look of gratitude before. This was where the man felt obligated to pay her back. This was what happened just before everything tumbled down. It was what happened when you allowed yourself to forget that you were no good at loving a man. But if you were going to regret losing a man, shouldn't you at least have something more to lose?

"I don't regret a thing," she said solemnly. "I'd do it all again. Everything. *Everything.* I'd do more."

The smile disappeared. His eyes turned fierce. He didn't say a word, but he held out his hand. She slid hers into his, and he led her out of the lobby and down the hallway.

Alex's words echoed through Wyatt's mind. Heat flowed through him. Hunger for her overcame him.

That was it. He was only human, and this woman, this maddeningly wonderful, vital woman…

He stopped, turned, and gazed down into her eyes. "I'm taking you to my apartment, Alex. I need to be alone with you. If you don't want to come with me, say so. I'll escort you to your room and we'll pretend that I never intended to make love with you, even though I'm dying for you. I'll return you to San Diego just as untouched as you arrived here, and—"

"No, I don't want to be untouched," she said, rising on her toes and kissing him. "The calendar dates will all be crossed off soon, and I am not going home without this. I'm done fighting not to want this. And I'm done counting. Let's leap."

She kissed him again, and when the elevator stopped, he carried her into his room, right to the bed, and fell down with her into the softness.

Finally, finally, he was going to have her. Maybe then he could get her out of his system.

So he kissed her. As much as he wanted. He flicked open the neckline-to-hem buttons on the pretty red dress she'd been wearing, and as she lay revealed to him, her red underthings a perfect contrast to the cream of her skin, he gazed at her. As much as he wanted.

Then he took what he wanted. Her mouth.

She sighed and kissed him back.

He nuzzled her cheeks, her chin, the hollow of her neck.

Alex gasped and reached to grasp the lapels of his jacket, peeling it down to his elbows in one quick move. He shrugged out of it.

He skimmed his hands down her sides from curve to curve.

She fumbled with his shirt, and he ripped it open and off. He finished undressing, and as he moved back to the bed she rose onto her knees, slipped her arms from the sleeves of the dress and moved on her knees to the side of the bed.

"I have to see all of you," he said, removing the little scraps of silk and lowering her back to the bed. She was soft and warm and jasmine-scented, and everything he wanted.

She met him kiss for kiss. "When this is over, I don't want you to be sorry," she said.

He smiled against her skin and breathed in. "That's supposed to be my line."

"This time it's mine."

"You think I could be sorry for this?" He kissed her again, touched her everywhere. He drank in her moan, licked her lips as she sighed.

When she was ready, he rose over her. She looked up at him, waiting. It was a look of…he couldn't translate that look. A second of concern slid through him.

"Are you regretting, Alex? Reconsidering?"

She slowly shook her head and smiled. "I'm savoring," she said. "I'm anticipating." She moved closer, her skin touching his.

His entire body turned to mindless heat and speed and need and…

"Alex," he said, biting off the word.

"Wyatt?" she said, uncertainty in her voice. "Are *you* reconsidering?"

"I'm counting," he said, trying to slow down. "I'm trying to go slow for you."

She slid her hands up his body, placed his hands on *her* body. "Don't try to go slow. Don't count. Love me now. Leap."

It was the last word he remembered. He leaped. He fell into the most wonderful sensation of his life.

When he woke, it was dark. The middle of the night.

Alex was gone.

There was a note on the table by the side of the bed.

I don't want anyone to accuse you of seducing the hired help. Thank you for leaping. And for hiring me. You've made all my dreams possible.

Wyatt blinked. He ran one hand through his hair. He swore beneath his breath. That polite little note. What did it mean?

It meant, he knew darn well, that he had had her and he had lost her. Just as he'd known he would.

In the past, with any other woman, it wouldn't have mattered. He wouldn't ever have left a polite note because it would have been understood from the start that making love didn't really mean making love.

But Alex wouldn't be that way. She'd worry about him feeling guilty. She'd worry about a lot of things. And she'd want to be sure that there were no bad feelings afterwards.

She was a woman who cared about people's feelings, who saved others. Today she'd helped him see that he didn't need to be a loner or hide from friendship. Tonight she'd made love with him and then made sure that he would feel no guilt. She was a fixer, a doer, who threw herself into everything headfirst.

She was, he realized, the woman he loved. The *only* woman he had ever loved. And her dreams were all focused elsewhere—not here, not with him. What should he do about that?

Let her go. Let her dream, he told himself.

He wanted to do that. He'd lived without love for so long it should be easy. But nothing with Alex was ever easy, he realized.

He also realized something else. No man had ever risked it all for her. She had walked through fire for men and been left sitting in the ashes when everything was over. No one had ever walked through fire for her.

That was just...

"Unacceptable," he said aloud. Completely unacceptable.

Alex's heart was in shreds. She didn't regret making love with Wyatt for one second, except that it made it so much more difficult to leave him now.

And she had to go. Belinda was back. Wyatt didn't need an extra concierge. Besides, what would be the good in staying after last night?

She just wasn't that good an actress. He would know. At the very least, Randy would notice. He might tell. And Wyatt would beat himself up. Hadn't she been told how much he hated hurting people?

That was why she was sitting here, bags packed. She had scrubbed her face with cold water and put her make-up on, then cried it off. Now, finally, after washing her face and applying her make-up again, she looked close to normal. Hopefully she could say some very quick goodbyes and duck into a cab. If she could make it that far, then Wyatt wouldn't know. That would have to be her only goal for now. *Keep your secret now, tears later, Lowell*, she coached herself.

With that order, she took a deep breath, left her room for the last time and headed down to the lobby. As she exited the elevator, the hotel seemed strangely quiet, with only the murmurs of a few guests as they passed by breaking the silence. But when she stepped into the lobby, everyone was there. Or at least it looked like everyone. Most of the employees. And Wyatt.

He stared at the bag she held in her hand.

"What's going on?" she asked.

"You're leaving."

She bit her lip. "Yes. It's time. I need to go." But she wanted nothing more than to run to him.

"I know. I knew it couldn't last forever. Even though I wish that it could." He stared into her eyes, and then he went down on one knee right in the middle of the crowded lobby.

"Wyatt? Are you okay? Wyatt?"

"I'm better than I've ever been in some ways, Alex. And all because of you."

"Did we…did you win, then?" Her voice was a choked whisper.

"I won. I don't know about the hotel yet. But here in this city, where anything can happen, something wonderful happened to me. You came into my lobby and you taught me about possibilities and friendship and—"

His deep voice seemed to break. He looked down for a minute. When he looked up again his eyes were fierce and glittering and…

"You taught me that I didn't have to hide inside myself all the time, that I could take chances with my heart. The lives of everyone here in this room have been changed by you. We were going along, picking up our accolades, doing a good job, and then you came along and showed us how to put our hearts into everything we did."

"We'll never forget you, Alex," Jenna said suddenly, and the room was suddenly less hushed as other people chimed in. But then they all turned to Wyatt, and were suddenly silent.

"*I'll* never forget you," he told her. "And I want you to know that if you're ever looking for a home again, if you ever need a place to go, you have one here. No work required."

Alex stared down at him, her heart in her throat. A lone tear escaped her lashes and she walked up to him. "You're breaking my heart."

"That wasn't what I wanted to do. At all."

Alex cupped her palm against his cheek. "What did you want to do?" she whispered. "Wyatt, I don't want you to do or say anything you'll regret."

He grasped her hand and touched his lips to her fingertips. "I could never regret anything I ever did with you. And what I wanted was to tell you publicly, so you'll never doubt that I mean it, is that there is one man you helped who didn't just feel grateful when the day was done. One man who loved you with every ounce of his being. Even if I have to let you go, even if I look like a fool for telling a woman who's leaving me that I love her, I'm telling *you*, Alexandra Lowell. You crept into my heart and I'm never going to stop loving you, no matter where you are."

Alex's heart overflowed. Somewhere she heard the snap of a camera, and she turned. "Don't print that. I don't want anyone to think Wyatt is…crazy just because he's down on his knees."

He smiled, a slow, sad smile. "I *am* crazy, Alex. And you're not helping. You could at least tell me that you'll think of me now and then."

"Wyatt—" Her voice broke; she wrapped her arms around his neck, sinking to her knees. "I couldn't *not* think about you. Every day. Every hour. How could I forget you when I love you so much? And you're driving me crazy, too."

"In what way?"

"You could…you could at least ask me not to go."

He closed his eyes tightly, pulled her against him. Tightly. "Don't go, Alex," he whispered against her hair. "Please stay. Marry me. Love me."

She launched herself against him so forcefully that they went tumbling backward, and she ended up sprawled across his chest with one of his arms wrapped around her. "Yes, yes and *yes*. I love San Diego, but I can visit. I can open a shop here, where you are, where my home and my heart is." She kissed his chest right over his heart.

Another camera snapped. "That had *so* better not end up in the newspaper," Alex said, while smiling down at Wyatt. "Something like that could cost McKendrick's the award."

"Well, the award wouldn't have mattered if Wyatt had sold the hotel," someone said. "That's what he said he was going to do."

Alex raised her head and frowned down at Wyatt. "Why would you have done that?"

He put one arm behind his head and lay back, staring into her eyes. "I was prepared to follow you if you were determined to go. If you wouldn't have minded a stubborn hotelier hanging around, that is."

She snapped her head up, raising her chin. "I would have minded you selling this place very much. What would McKendrick's be without McKendrick to run it? Although that *is* the most romantic thing anyone's ever said to me. And I loved hearing you say it."

He kissed her. "Let's get married this weekend."

"That's what I like—a man of action."

"You can choose the place."

She kissed *him*. "I choose the Haven."

He laughed, a deep, hearty, wonderful laugh. "You always liked a challenge. We'll never get it done in time."

"Oh, yes, we will. We have friends. *You* have friends."

"I do. And you have family here. A home," he said, indicating the roof high over their heads. "We'll manage."

As they lay there Randy came forward, carrying a bag.

"What's this?" Wyatt asked.

"My winnings. Your wedding present," Randy said. "When it comes down to the wire, I find I can't profit off my friends. But I won the bet," he told Alex as he opened the bag, threw its contents in the air and let the dollars rain down. "I always knew that if Wyatt ever fell in love you would be the one."

"She was always the one," Wyatt agreed. "From the first moment I saw her, she stole my heart."

Alex smiled. She looked at the money lying around them. "Well, I think this would be enough for a very nice party for our McKendrick's family, don't you think, Wyatt?"

"You always have the best ideas, my love."

She rested her arms on his chest and leaned closer. "I have another good idea, too."

"What is it?"

"Kiss me again, Wyatt."

"Best idea ever," he said, sitting up gracefully and folding her into his arms. "I can't believe I didn't think of it."

"You would have. In time."

"I think you're right." And he kissed her one more time.

Two evenings later, Alex stood at the back of the short aisle of the chapel, waiting to meet Wyatt. All their friends had, indeed, worked a miracle. The tiny building was lit by hundreds of candles, their light bouncing off the creamy walls. The stars shone through the deep open windows. The rugged pews were draped in white satin, and the honeyed floors were strewn with blood-red roses.

It was so beautiful. But what mattered more was that her friends were there. Jayne, Molly and Serena smiled up at her.

"Be happy," Jayne had said before the ceremony.

"She is," Molly had answered. "You can see it in her eyes."

"And she's loved," Serena had added. "You can see it in every look he gives her."

Katrina and Beverly sat next to Randy, who had brought Wyatt and Alex a newspaper this morning that contained an announcement that McKendrick's had nosed past Champagne for the award. The story had commented on the hotel's tasteful décor, its enthusiastic and welcoming staff and exciting events.

"Thank goodness the photo is of the hotel and not of the two of us lying together on the floor of the lobby," she'd teased.

"Oh, I don't know. I'm rather fond of that photo. Jenna told me I could have one for my office."

Alex had shrieked.

"Or our bedroom," he'd conceded, with a wink and a kiss.

But all the teasing and kissing was over now, and Alex lifted her chin and gazed down the aisle to where Wyatt waited, looking tall and gorgeous, a man *any* woman would love to share her life and her bed with.

The lone wolf, Alex couldn't help thinking as she walked toward him. He'd been alone—by choice—for a long time. His proposal had been sudden, made soon after a euphoric, chaotic day. Those good feelings didn't always last, as she well knew, especially when gratitude was thrown into the mix. And it *had* only been two days since Wyatt had proposed. Was there a chance he would change his mind eventually? Would he miss his solitary life, or feel trapped by the promises he'd made? And if he did…if he did…

Would he even tell her? He'd always been so careful about not hurting her… A sudden frisson of fear rippled through her.

Alex smiled at Jayne and Molly, and at Serena, seated with her husband, Jonas, even as doubts assailed her.

Then she was walking down the aisle again. She was by Wyatt's side. Her love. Her heart. The man she wanted to be with forever. And yet…

She turned to him and rose on her toes, putting her lips near his ear. "If you want to run, love, now's the time to go."

He gazed down at her, an intimidating expression in his eyes. She wasn't intimidated, only worried.

"You're offering me my freedom, Alexandra?" he asked.

She swallowed. "If you want it, yes."

A slow smile lifted his lips. He swept her into his arms. "What I want is you. The only place I want to run is *to* you." He kissed her lips, long and deep and slowly.

Every doubt and fear in Alex's heart flew away. She kissed

him back with all the love in her heart. Her bouquet of blood-red roses dropped to the floor.

Behind her someone laughed. "It's highly irregular for the kisses to come *before* the wedding," they joked.

Alex smiled into Wyatt's eyes. "There's not going to be anything regular or ordinary about *this* marriage," she said, loudly enough for everyone to hear. "Kiss me again, Wyatt."

He did. With fervor.

"Thank goodness you had the good sense to choose a lot of fools before I came along, Alex. I would have hated it if I hadn't gotten to be the one to marry you and love you and sleep with you and have children with you."

"I would have hated that, too. So much. Let's get married, Wyatt," she said.

"The sooner the better. I want to be your husband from here to eternity, and I'd like to start that right now," he said, taking her in his arms again, to the delight of all those assembled in the chapel.

It *was* a less than conventional wedding. The bouquet had to be gathered up again so that it could be tossed later. There was dancing in the aisles when the ceremony was over. There were kisses where there weren't supposed to be kisses.

"The perfect wedding," Alex said with a sigh.

"To my perfect bride." And, lifting her against his heart, Wyatt McKendrick carried her away to his lair at the pinnacle of his hotel, in the heart of the city that had brought them together on one wild weekend that had turned golden.

HARLEQUIN Romance.

Coming Next Month

Available July 13, 2010

#4177 A WISH AND A WEDDING
Margaret Way and Melissa James

#4178 THE BRIDESMAID'S SECRET
Fiona Harper
The Brides of Bella Rosa

#4179 MAID FOR THE MILLIONAIRE
Susan Meier
Housekeepers Say I Do!

#4180 SOS: CONVENIENT HUSBAND REQUIRED
Liz Fielding

#4181 VEGAS PREGNANCY SURPRISE
Shirley Jump
Girls' Weekend in Vegas

#4182 WINNING A GROOM IN 10 DATES
Cara Colter
The Fun Factor

HARLEQUIN®

A *Romance*

FOR EVERY MOOD™

Spotlight on
Heart & Home

Heartwarming romances
where love can happen
right when you least expect it.

See the next page to enjoy a sneak peek
from Silhouette Special Edition®,
a Heart and Home series.

*Introducing MCFARLANE'S PERFECT BRIDE
by USA TODAY bestselling author Christine Rimmer,
from Silhouette Special Edition®.*

Entranced. Captivated. Enchanted.

Connor sat across the table from Tori Jones and
couldn't help thinking that those words exactly described
what effect the small-town schoolteacher had on him.
He might as well stop trying to tell himself he wasn't
interested. He was powerfully drawn to her.

Clearly, he should have dated more when he was
younger.

There had been a couple of other women since Jennifer
had walked out on him. But he had never been entranced.
Or captivated. Or enchanted.

Until now.

He wanted her—*her,* Tori Jones, in particular. Not just
someone suitably attractive and well-bred, as Jennifer had
been. Not just someone sophisticated, sexually exciting
and discreet, which pretty much described the two women
he'd dated after his marriage crashed and burned.

It came to him that he…he *liked* this woman. And that
was new to him. He liked her quick wit, her wisdom and
her big heart. He liked the passion in her voice when she
talked about things she believed in.

He liked *her.* And suddenly it mattered all out of
proportion that she might like him, too.

Was he losing it? He couldn't help but wonder. Was
he cracking under the strain—of the soured economy, the
McFarlane House setbacks, his divorce, the scary changes
in his son? Of the changes he'd decided he needed to make
in his life and himself?

Strangely, right then, on his first date with Tori Jones, he didn't care if he just might be going over the edge. He was having a great time—having *fun,* of all things—and he didn't want it to end.

*Is Connor finally able to admit his feelings to Tori,
and are they reciprocated?
Find out in M*cFARLANE'S PERFECT BRIDE
by USA TODAY *bestselling author Christine Rimmer.
Available July 2010,
only from Silhouette Special Edition®.*

Bestselling Harlequin Presents® author

Penny Jordan

brings you an exciting new trilogy...

Needed:
THE WORLD'S MOST
ELIGIBLE
BILLIONAIRES

Three penniless sisters:
how far will they go to save the ones they love?

Lizzie, Charley and Ruby refuse to drown in their debts.
And three of the richest, most ruthless men in the world
are about to enter their lives. Pure, proud but penniless,
how far will these sisters go to save the ones they love?

Look out for

Lizzie's story—THE WEALTHY GREEK'S
CONTRACT WIFE, July

Charley's story—THE ITALIAN DUKE'S
VIRGIN MISTRESS, August

Ruby's story—MARRIAGE: TO CLAIM HIS TWINS,
September

www.eHarlequin.com

HP12927